T0278981

VITA

NUOVA

ALSO BY JOSEPH LUZZI

Dante's "Divine Comedy":
A Biography

Botticelli's Secret: The Lost
Drawings and the Rediscovery
of the Renaissance

In a Dark Wood: What Dante
Taught Me About Grief, Healing,
and the Mysteries of Love

My Two Italies

A Cinema of Poetry: Aesthetics
of the Italian Art Film

Romantic Europe and the Ghost
of Italy

EDITED BY JOSEPH LUZZI

Italian Cinema: From the Silent
Screen to the Digital Image

VITA

NUOVA

DANTE

ALIGHIERI

Translated by

JOSEPH LUZZI

Liveright Publishing Corporation

A Division of W. W. Norton & Company
Independent Publishers Since 1923

Copyright © 2025 by Joseph Luzzi

All rights reserved
Printed in the United States of America
First Edition

For information about permission to reproduce selections from this book,
write to Permissions, Liveright Publishing Corporation, a division of
W. W. Norton & Company, Inc., 500 Fifth Avenue, New York, NY 10110

For information about special discounts for bulk purchases, please
contact W. W. Norton Special Sales at specialsales@wwnorton.com or
800-233-4830

Manufacturing by Versa Press
Book design by Marysarah Quinn
Production manager: Julia Druskin

ISBN 978-1-324-09552-1

Liveright Publishing Corporation, 500 Fifth Avenue, New York, N.Y. 10110
www.wwnorton.com

W. W. Norton & Company Ltd., 15 Carlisle Street, London W1D 3BS

1 2 3 4 5 6 7 8 9 0

For my daughter

Annabel Beatrice Luzzi

Un riso de l'universo

A smile of the universe

—DANTE, *PARADISO*

Dante understood the secret things of love . . .

—PERCY BYSSHE SHELLEY

CONTENTS

TRANSLATOR'S PREFACE

No words infused with music can be translated
without destroying their sweetness and harmony.

—DANTE, *Convivio*

THESE WORDS have proven eerily prophetic for the author who coined them. While other ancient and medieval masterpieces have been translated into modern versions that have become classics in their own regard, the music of Dante's poetry can feel inaccessible to today's readers. He wrote his most celebrated work, the *Commedia*, in an intensely idiomatic, rhyme-rich Tuscan with a surging *terza rima* meter that gives this epic poem its galloping energy—a unique rhythm that's difficult to reproduce in rhyme-poor English separated from Dante's vernacular by centuries.[1] The content of Dante's writing presents an even bigger problem. Dante was more Milton than Shakespeare: an intensely scholarly author, he filled his verses with allusions to ancient, biblical, and contemporary medieval writing, tackling a range of theological, philosophical, political, and historical issues. The last transcendentally great translation of the *Commedia* is, in my view, from as far back as 1867 and by Henry Wadsworth Longfellow.

He had the two necessary ingredients to make Dante's original come alive. First, he was a poet, one of the best and most widely read in nineteenth-century America. And he was an accomplished scholar of Italian as well, spending much of his career at Harvard as a renowned professor of modern languages.

Similarly, I believe that for the last "classic" translation of the *Vita Nuova* in English, one must go back to the Pre-Raphaelite painter and poet Dante Gabriel Rossetti and his 1861 edition. Of the *Vita Nuova*'s many English translators, Rossetti alone has been able to recreate the music of Dante's original while reproducing the historical detail of his words and the resonance of his cultural context. Most important, he managed to convey the raw, disruptive, and hallucinatory elements of a work that combines elements as diverse as earthly love, blinding grief, and intimations of eternal grace.[2] Despite the majesty of this Pre-Raphaelite *Vita Nuova*, its English is too dated and its idiosyncratic structure too loose to serve today's readers.[3] A gifted poet and artist in his own right, Rossetti was at times too creative for his own good when it came to rendering the *Vita Nuova* into English, refusing to translate what he believed were its more prosaic, less exalted—but essential[4]—elements, including its chapter divisions. He even relegated the translation of the text's explanatory sections, where Dante says how and why he wrote his poems, to his brother, William Michael Rossetti.

In the etymological spirit of the word "translation,"

this volume aims to "carry over" Dante's unusual blend of music and meaning from the Middle Ages into the present. Unlike *The Divine Comedy*, which represents the mature Dante at the height of his powers and writing in a language of otherworldly precision and concision (Borges says it takes a modern novel hundreds of pages to do what Dante can achieve in a handful of verses[5]), the *Vita Nuova*'s original can seem winding, circuitous, and repetitive. Put simply, Dante the young poet is far superior to Dante the young prose writer, especially in the rather workmanlike explanations that Dante affixes to each of the delicate poems in the *Vita Nuova*. In seeking that fine balance between poetry and prose, and in navigating that historical divide between Dante's world and our own, I have aimed for the following qualities.

1. READABILITY AND ACCESSIBILITY

My primary goal has been to create a lively and idiomatic translation of Dante's work that resonates with contemporary readers. To that end, I try to find the modern equivalents for Dante's medieval poetry and prose. So I broke up Dante's long single sentences into smaller units, while at the same time trying to maintain the cascading flow of the original. I also eliminated what are now unnecessary connectives like the conjunction *e* ("and"), adjective *sopraddetto* (the clunky "above-mentioned"), and adverb *poi* ("then"). Similarly, at times I omitted Dante's authorial interjections at the beginning of sentences like *dico che* ("let me say") when I felt that including them would seem cumbersome or awkward. In this same spirit, I transformed archaic-sounding constructions like *molto virtuosamente* ("most virtuously") into more colloquial forms. My drive for idiomatic fluency in English also prompted me to translate Dante's frequent use of the superlative—after all, the *Vita Nuova* is a youthful text prone to lexical exuberance—in more muted keys. For example, when Dante writes "*dolcissimo*" in chapter 9 to describe the lord of Love, it seemed sufficient to render that as "sweet" without affixing a weak adverb like "very" or, worse, lapsing into the archaic-sounding "most sweet" or "sweetest." And while many editions of the *Vita Nuova* tend to use a hanging indent (which indents all lines of a stanza except for the first), I have opted for the more contemporary practice of indenting only the first stanza line. Similarly, I have deferred to the tradition in English of capitalizing the first letter of each word beginning a new line of poetry.

Finally, and fittingly, a word on Beatrice: Dante often refers to her by code or periphrasis, as the *gentilissima*, "most gracious one," source of *beatitudine*, "bliss," and so on. At times, I made the text a bit less secretive and hermetic by interspersing Beatrice's name alongside these coded references, to help the reader follow the thread of Dante's ongoing elegy to his Florentine paramour. My reasoning here is that the *Vita Nuova* is mysterious enough without the added burden of forcing the reader to decipher personal shout-outs that come across much more clearly in the gendered inflections of Italian than they do in English. I will say more below on this issue of grammatical inflection in the original Tuscan—and the lack thereof in English— and its implications for my translation.

2. HISTORICAL ACCURACY

Perhaps the greatest challenge to translating Dante in a contemporary manner is to do so without losing the historical specificity and meaning of his own language. Drawing on my training in Italian studies and knowledge of the original Tuscan language, I have sought to make the transition from Dante's medieval text to modern English in a way that still retains the resonance and meaning of the original. So I have rendered Dante's Tuscan in "palimpsestic" fashion: I hope the reader will be able to detect, in my English, the essence and character of the original, as though through a transparent linguistic film placed over the text written in Dante's hand. For example, I translate *beatitudine* not as its cognate, the accurate but overwrought-sounding "beatitude," nor as the more modern but vague and unspecific "happiness." I chose "bliss" because it is modern-sounding enough, yet it also retains that necessary connotation of spiritual plentitude—after all, Dante uses the term to describe his sainted Beatrice— inherent in "beatitude" but absent in "happiness."

Another key word requiring special lexical attention is *donna*, which in Dante's age signified a "lady" of high rank, often nobility, as opposed to the less socially exalted world of the *femmina*, "female," who could be from the poor and working classes. Translators of *donna* have typically opted for "lady" because of its suggestion of status, but I found that using that term exclusively gives off a fussy, antiquated air.[6] So I alternated between the two English terms, employing "lady" often enough to indicate the quality of elevated class, but also interspersing the more colloquial "woman" in the spirit of contemporary usage. I realize this "splicing" effect divides Dante's single term into two signifiers, but the English target language seemed to call for a strategy that updated *donna* to twenty-first-century conventions while also retaining its original medieval meaning.

3. METRICAL FORM

My overarching goal is to give Dante's poetry a metrical structure and musical rhythm in English. In the spirit of an illustrious predecessor like Rossetti, I opted for the unstressed/stressed rhythm of iambs, usually in tetrameter to express the compactness and precision of Dante's sleek original. In a few cases like the first poem in the *Vita Nuova*, "A ciascun'alma presa," "To every captive soul," and the legendary canzone "Donne ch'avete intelletto d'amore," "Ladies who are intelligent in love," I used iambic pentameter, in response to what

I felt was the expansiveness and fullness of the lines. Though my general structure was in tetrameter, I also occasionally interspersed a five-beat line when the usual four beats felt either too compressed or insufficient to capture the verse's full range of meaning. Similarly, when Dante's line is particularly compact, I have opted for the occasional trimetric English rendering.

Unlike Dante's original, my verse translations have no rhyme scheme, on the grounds that rhyme-poor English can sound forced and singsongy to a contemporary ear when laced into rhyming tercets. Eschewing rhyme, I have nonetheless hewn, as closely as possible, to the linear flow of Dante's original. Throughout, I have kept in mind Milton's claim about "rhyme being no necessary adjunct or true ornament of poem or good verse" in my quest for an understated music in English that conjures the rhythm and flow of the original Tuscan.[7]

4. STRUCTURAL INTEGRITY

Paragraph breaks are infrequent in Dante's original Tuscan, and translators have taken differing approaches to this challenge of his unbroken prose. My own practice, in the interest of readability, is to insert breaks at junctures where I believe the text is switching gears, and where the reader could use a visual pause or cue to indicate that transition. As a writer intensely aware of his *lettori*, readers—Dante addresses them no less than twenty times in *The Divine Comedy*—I believe that he would approve of my slight recalibration of his text into more user-friendly paragraphs.

As with the paragraphs, I broke up some of Dante's longer sentences into more concise and manageable syntactic units. Italian in general tends to have lengthier and more involved sentences than English: it is a highly inflected language, with gender and number—there are seven ways to say "the" alone,[8] as well as much more dramatic conjugations of verbs than in English. Because of these inflections, one can string together longer sentences in Italian and still have a good sense of how the different clauses relate to one another. Not so in English. Since it does not indicate gender, and because there are only slight differences in its conjugations (for example, "I go," "you go," "he/she goes," etc.), it is generally wise to be concise and economical in usage and avoid baroque structures. A brilliant poet even in his youth, Dante could also be a deft prose craftsman: his sentences are lucid, his language precise, and his imagery evocative. Reducing the length of his sentences and the number of his clauses seemed like the best way to capture the force of his original prose.

As with the paragraphs, so with the poems: in Dante's original, there are no spaces between stanzas, even in an extremely long canzone like "Ladies who are intelligent in love." In the interest of readability, and to employ a more modern technique, I inserted stanza breaks and began lines with capitals when it felt like doing so was in the spirit of the *Vita Nuova*, if not its letter.

5. CLARITY AND TRANSPARENCY

I translated Dante's Latin passages into English. I realize that translators will often leave foreign words untranslated to distinguish them from the translated original, but I abandoned this practice for a simple reason: today's reader is unlikely to be as fluent in Latin as the one in Dante's age. Latin was the lingua franca for educated medieval audiences, who would have easily grasped the meaning of Dante's Latin references. That desired effect of instant recognition for today's reader could be obtained only by transforming the Latin into English. Similarly, in certain instances Dante invokes arcane numerological or chronological references that, again, the reader of his time would have recognized but today's may not. I have rendered these passages in their current equivalents.

Of course, it is one thing to outline my principles and general approach to the *Vita Nuova*, and it is another thing for the reader to judge if the actual translation is a success. Working on the *Vita Nuova* has been at once humbling and exhilarating. The complexities of the text, often hidden behind a beguiling sense of youthful exuberance and what can seem, to the naked eye, its reliance on now obsolete formulas or protocols, have given me a strong sense of solidarity with the distinguished fellow translators who have also thrown their hat into this literary ring. In the end, Dante will always be one step ahead of all of us who translate him. The best one can hope for is to create pleasing, useful, and accurate approximations of his towering original. Yet how thrilling it is to encounter this magical work in its raw and unmediated form. It is above all that transporting energy, mystery, and strangeness of the original that I try to bring to the reader. Early in the *Vita Nuova*, Dante describes Beatrice appearing to him naked in a dream, covered only by a veil. That's what translating the *Vita Nuova* can feel like: the text comes to you in its raw and unadorned Tuscan, covered by a veil of time and linguistic difference that you try to render transparent as you layer it with new words.

INTRODUCTION

THE *VITA NUOVA*, written between 1292 and 1295[9] and referred to by Dante as his *libello*, "little book," has had an outsized impact on English readers disproportionate to its slight form. Wallace Stevens called it "one of the great documents of Christianity," and the Pre-Raphaelite Brotherhood of Dante Gabriel Rossetti in Victorian England considered it a bible, celebrating its medieval world and casting its imagery into magnificent paintings that exude an unusual mix of the sensual and spiritual. Allusions to Dante's early autobiography appear in such major works as James Joyce's *A Portrait of the Artist as a Young Man*, Percy Bysshe Shelley's "A Defence of Poetry," and D. M. Thomas's *The White Hotel*, among many others. In 2009, the *Vita Nuova* premiered as an opera by Vladimir Martynov in New York; less grandly, it was referenced in a 1999 episode of the television show *Star Trek: Voyager*. That same year, Nobel laureate Louise Glück wrote the poem "Vita Nova," a meditation on love and old age ("Surely spring has been returned to me, this time / not as a lover but a messenger of death"[10]), both a contrast and an homage to Dante's emphatically youthful text. In the film *Hannibal* from 2001, Dr. Hannibal Lecter creepily watches an opera in Florence called *Vide Cor Tuum* (*Behold Your Heart*), which is based on the *Vita Nuova*'s haunting— and fittingly cannibalistic—sonnet "To every captive soul." More recently, Allegra Goodman's short story "La Vita Nuova" offered this spright summary of the *libello*:

> "La Vita Nuova" explained how to become a great poet. The secret was to fall in love with a perfect girl but never speak to her. You should weep instead. You should pretend that you love someone else. You should write sonnets in three parts. Your perfect girl should die.[11]

This global, public impact of the *Vita Nuova* would have likely surprised the author of what was intended to be a local, private book. Almost entirely devoid of names, dates, and geographical markers, the *Vita Nuova* ostensibly organizes Dante's early poems around the story of how he first met his muse Beatrice Portinari and fell under her spell. But, as Dante would put it, the reader should look beneath the literal surface for allegorical, moral, and celestial undercurrents.[12] Love story, instruction manual, spiritual journey—all these and much more factor into the book's forty-two short chapters. Dante called the *Vita Nuova* the "new life" to signify the cataclysmic effect of meeting Beatrice, the woman who divided his life and career into a before and after. The title is apt for many other reasons. It was "new" or unusual as a literary form, the prosimetrum, a mix of prose and poetry that had formal antecedents in such ancient works as Petronius's *Satyricon* (first century AD) and Boethius's *De consolatione philosophiae* (*The Consolation of Philosophy*, AD 523). It was new also because of the strange, irruptive quality of its narrative voice and authorial persona, who by book's end would systematically dismantle the core values of that same youthful poetry that had shaped him. Last, it was new because Dante was after more than the story of a local poet's infatuation with a local girl and the poetic apprenticeship that accompanied it. It is impossible to map the scope of Dante's towering ambition. Suffice it to say that even as a young poet finding his voice and his way in the world of letters, he dreamed big. In this case, his aim was no less than to give his Tuscan dialect a tradition that made it worthy of comparison to the legendary lyrics of ancient Rome.

Despite the library of responses the *Vita Nuova* has elicited over the centuries, the work remains Dante's most mysterious. Not surprisingly, the word "essay" has long been associated with the attempts made by scholars, including some of the grandest names in Dante studies, to come to terms with the seemingly inscrutable *Vita Nuova*.[13] As one commentator put it astutely, even professional critics have wished to signal their "tentative, noncomprehensive approach" to a work that by its nature resists clarity and closure.[14] The term "essay" is indeed apt, and not just because it suggests the difficulty of gaining traction on this unpredictable medieval book. As we will see, the *Vita Nuova* itself becomes "essayistic" when Dante faces the crisis of Beatrice's death—which, not incidentally, will lead to both his break with the poetic movement that had formed him and, more important, his discovery of his ultimate vocation as a writer. This journey to the essayistic core of the work centers on six key themes that took seed in the *Vita Nuova* and would remain lifelong obsessions for Dante.

1. RETHINKING LOVE

Dante's path to poetic and personal maturity had a long gestation period and inspired his own endless autobiographical commentary. As one would guess, it also began with Beatrice. In a signature moment early in the *Vita Nuova*, chapter 3, the intense eighteen-year-old protagonist Dante approaches the familiar river at the center of his city—without naming either the Arno or Florence. Perhaps he is on his way to visit a friend or attend a lecture, maybe even share poems with his inner circle of fellow *rimatori*, versifiers in the Tuscan dialect. He is alone, as the youth tends to be, devoted to his studies of rhetoric, theology, philosophy, and science, and restricting his social life to the city's elite. Here is Dante's depiction of the scene:

After so much time had passed that it had been exactly nine years since the appearance of the gracious Beatrice, this miraculous woman once again appeared to me, dressed in the purest white and standing in between two older ladies. Crossing the street, she glanced toward where I stood agitated, and with her indescribable courtesy, which today is rewarded in heaven, she greeted me so virtuously that I felt as though I were witnessing the very limits of bliss.[15]

The world treated men and women very differently at the time, but the lives of the teenage Dante and Beatrice were actually quite similar. They belonged to the same demographic of their city's rigid socioeconomic ladder—though Beatrice stood on a higher rung. Their families were invited to the same parties, including the one where they had allegedly first met, nine years earlier.[16] Their friends knew one another; their future spouses would come from the same circle; they mourned the same loved ones. These were kids from the same metaphysical block.

In natural terms, the locking of gazes between the lover Dante and his beloved Beatrice in *Vita Nuova* 3 differs little from today. Like all in the throes of attraction, Dante likely felt a bodily charge drawing him to the lovely Beatrice, whom he would list as one of Florence's most beautiful women in his poem "Guido i' vorrei" ("O Guido, how I wish") from 1292. The reader senses the physical element of desire, perhaps even Dante's yearning for the touch and feel of the person who has stimulated his passion. But, then as now, the natural must contend with the social. What could Dante do with this sensation of love and desire? Pursue a passing affair, hazard a relationship, transform passion into the affection of friendship—or domesticate it with marriage? His choice was simple: sublimation at all costs. In his literary milieu, to desire the beloved was never to attain her, and certainly not marry her. A lodestone for Dante and his fellow *fedeli d'Amore*, Love's faithful, was Andreas Capellanus's *De amore* (*The Art of Courtly Love*; 1186–90), which saw love and marriage as not merely incidentally related, but as actually antithetical. Marriages in Dante's noble world were generally arranged. Hence his childhood engagement to Gemma Donati, who became his wife when he turned thirty, a full eighteen years after the initial betrothal. Beatrice would wed the banker and fellow plutocrat Simone Bardi in 1287, four years after her teenage encounter with Dante. The true lover, in Dante's time, worshipped from afar, not up close. Proof of this can be gleaned from Dante's great poem, *The Divine Comedy*: 14,233 lines, all written for the elusive, untouchable Beatrice. And Gemma? Not a single verse for the woman who bore him at least three children, possibly four,[17] and steadfastly endured twenty years of his exile.

To imagine Dante watching Beatrice pass by the

Arno is similar to staring at the two figures emblazoned on Keats's ancient urn:

When old age shall this generation waste,
*   Thou shalt remain, in midst of other woe*
Than ours, a friend to man, to whom thou say'st,
*   "Beauty is truth, truth beauty,—that is all*
*   Ye know on earth, and all ye need to know."*[18]

Truth and beauty were indeed one for the young author of the *Vita Nuova*, unlike the older and more moralistic Dante of the *Commedia*, whose suspicion of the seductive power of art led him, in *Inferno*, to condemn Paolo and Francesca's sensual reading of Arthurian romance.[19] Yet, by book's end, the *Vita Nuova* would reject the cliché of the adoring poet and his distant, anonymous muse. It even did something that, until then, no work had dared in the realm of love: imbue the object of affection and devotion with an individuality so distinct and irreplaceable that her loss sent Dante into paroxysms of grief that confounded social norms and inspired him to redefine love poetry. That loss, in the form of Beatrice's death, was only a remote, far-off possibility to the young, high-spirited teenager who crosses paths with his beloved by the Arno in chapter 3 of the *Vita Nuova*. Yet that adolescent encounter set in motion a new definition of love that would eventually reach its apotheosis, as was so often the case for Dante, in the soaring verses of his *Commedia*, which returned to—indeed, resurrected—Beatrice in a dramatically altered form.

2. MAPPING SOCIAL IDENTITY

Surprisingly, the *Vita Nuova* is also the transcript of a decidedly practical element that stood a world apart from the lover's sighs and sorrows: Dante's class anxieties.[20] Desperate to gain entry into the city's elite, the young poet realized he needed more than just his own native talent and vaulting ambition, so he set about cultivating the right kind of friends—especially the dedicatee of the *Vita Nuova*, Guido Cavalcanti. Dante worshipped Guido, nine years his senior, like an adoring younger brother. The Cavalcanti were *magnati* (magnates), among the handful of the city's wealthiest families who controlled its politics and set the tone for its social life. An accomplished philosopher and student of the natural sciences, Guido followed the latest intellectual developments in realms as far-flung as the Arab commentators on Aristotle.[21] He quickly grasped the secret meaning of Dante's first poem in the *Vita Nuova*, "A ciascun'alma presa," "To every captive soul," answering with a poem of his own, "Vedeste, al mio parere, onne valore," "I think all virtue came before your eyes." "Our friendship started when he learned that I was the one who had sent out the sonnet," Dante wrote. He could not resist adding that soon enough the meaning of his sonnet became self-evident to "even the most simpleminded," despite the cluelessness of his initial interlocutors. One of them, Dante da Maiano, actually suggested that the overheated Dante submerge his testicles in a cool bath to simmer down his libido.

Guido's influence is everywhere in the *Vita Nuova*, which contains such trademark Cavalcantian signifiers as *sospiri* (sighs) and *sbigottito* (bewildered) as well as verbal winks like the word *cavalcando*, a play on the name Cavalcanti that means "riding by horse." The extent of Dante's love for Guido—and the joy of Dante's entry into Guido's charmed circle—can be grasped from the poem "O Guido, how I wish":

> *O Guido, how I wish that you and me*
> *And Lapo too could be sent out by spell*
> *Upon a ship that winds would blow about*
> *The sea according to your will and mine.*

The lines exude the solidarity and affection binding Dante to Guido, one of the two founders of the sweet new style (*dolce stil novo*), a poetic movement of sorts devoted to exploring the devastating effects of love.[22] A good way to think about Dante's magical "boat of love" in "O Guido, how I wish"—and the circle of versifiers in the *Vita Nuova*—is as medieval Florence's version of a Dead Poets Society. Similar to the eponymous film from 1989 starring Robin Williams as John Keating, an English teacher at an exclusive boarding school who instructs his button-down pupils on how to live and love wildly through poetry, the young Dante in Florence ran with

an exclusive crowd dedicated to magnifying the sensa-
tions of emotional life through secret and coded literary
communication. They wrote for one another, pined for
the same group of muses, and, according to one scholar,
may even have taken mind-altering "love potions" at
their poetry-laced soirées.[23] Of course, Guido's name,
along with everyone else's, is never mentioned in the
Vita Nuova. It is a book meant only for those already in
the know.

Dante found ways to burnish the luster of his own
invisible name in the *Vita Nuova*. A similar motive
would compel him, later in the *Commedia*, to avoid men-
tioning his actual living relations and focus instead on
an illustrious forebear, Cacciaguida, a man of impec-
cable Florentine stock who participated in the twelfth-
century Second Crusade. The young Dante suffered
from a familiar problem in Italian social history, one
brilliantly depicted by Giuseppe Tomasi di Lampedusa
in *The Leopard* from 1958, a novel whose highborn but
cash-strapped protagonist is compelled to marry his
nephew Tancredi to the daughter of the wealthy but ple-
beian Don Calogero. Like the Leopard, Dante was rich
in name, but middling in assets. His father, a small-time
businessman who may have been buried in the *fosse*, pits
reserved for usurers and debtors,[24] died when Dante was
a child, leaving the family dependent on their meager
property holdings for income. Crucially, Dante insisted
on living off these precarious rents so that he could focus
on his writing and his studies. His profession as "author"

was thus intimately bound to his relatively high, but by no means stratospheric, socioeconomic standing. Daughter of the much wealthier Portinari, Beatrice was as aspirational a muse for Dante as Cavalcanti was as bosom friend. The luster of a beloved like Beatrice and a mentor like Guido brought refracted glory to a young poet desperate to scale the literary and social ladder.

3. EXPANDING THE AUDIENCE

The friendship between Dante and Guido, which began so beautifully, was ultimately doomed. For reasons not fully known—and despite the vast amount of scholarship on their relationship[25]—by the late 1290s the two had drifted apart. Politics was much to blame. Their Florence had long been riven by a civil war between the ruling, pro-papal Guelph party and their adversaries, the Ghibellines. The Guelphs splintered into two groups, the Blacks, which included the radical and irascible Cavalcanti, and the Whites, supported by the more moderate but equally tetchy Dante. In 1300, Guido's Black faction participated in a series of bloody attacks on the Whites that compelled the Guelph leadership and the city's six ruling priors to banish Cavalcanti from Florence to Sarzana, a swampy Tuscan town where Guido contracted malaria, dying soon afterward. One of the priors, the highest elected office in the city, was Dante. Astonishingly, he had signed the death warrant of his *primo amico*.

Despite the dramatic events that ended their friendship, more than politics divided Dante and Guido. Ultimately, they had different definitions of poetry and conflicting understandings of its cultural mission. Dante was far too restless and ambitious to settle for mere protégé status. Even within the *Vita Nuova*, tensions arose between the two poets about who their readers should be. Not long after Dante was accepted into Guido's inner circle, Dante made an unexpected decision: to write not for the local Dead Poets Society, but instead for a group that the latter treated merely as a means to an end—that is, as nameless sources of inspiration, interchangeable and thus generic: their female muses.

Vexed over his inability to communicate the depth of his love for Beatrice to her fellow highborn women ("We beg you to tell us where this bliss of yours resides," they ask Dante at one point), he shifted gears and began to write directly for them, instead of the usual elite male reader. Fittingly, this idea came to Dante when he was alone, unencumbered by the snares of society and separated from the distractions of the city:

> Then one day as I walked along a long path that went along a limpid stream, I suddenly felt the need to write a poem and began to think about how I would go about it. I felt that I should not speak of Beatrice unless I addressed my words to ladies—and not just any ladies but only those who are gracious and not run-of-the-mill. Then my tongue began to speak as

if moved by itself, uttering the words "Ladies who are
intelligent in love."

The seemingly anodyne gesture of replacing one
group of posh readers (rich, male poets) with another
(rich, learned females) was revolutionary. For the first
time in the *Vita Nuova*—and for arguably the first time
in Western literary history—a writer stepped outside
of his inexorably male and patriarchal realm to imag-
ine a group of women, the traditional object of liter-
ary inspiration but never its subject, as his intended
audience. By introducing his work to ladies with
knowledge of love, Dante affirmed his role as a cul-
tural emissary intent on expanding vernacular poetry's
reach—that same reach that the unabashedly elitist
Cavalcanti sought to limit.

4. CREATING CULTURE

As "Ladies who are intelligent in love" shows, despite
the erotic charge of his encounters with Beatrice, they
were always about more than passion. They also meant
finding new readers and new ways of writing about
love, new ventures into a burgeoning Tuscan literary
tradition. Such an attitude compelled Dante to create
magical figures like the imposing lord of Love who so
often appears in the *Vita Nuova*, sometimes to frighten
Dante, other times to support him as he wallows in the
throes of passion. This personification and irresistible

leap into allegory was just one of many practices, Dante argued, that made the poets like him the heirs of their great Latin predecessors:

> I believe that, to a certain degree, to write poetry in the vernacular is no different from writing it in Latin. To get a sense of just how brief the history of vernacular poetry is, you will not find a Provençal or Italian poem written more than 150 years ago. This is the reason a few poetic hacks gained renown, simply because they were the first to write in the dialect.
>
> The first poet who felt the need to write in the vernacular did so because he wanted his words to be understood by women who had great difficulty with Latin.

With the *Vita Nuova*, Dante embarked on a mission of elevating poetry in general—and the poets writing it—into the cultural pantheon. We can therefore think of the "project" of the *Vita Nuova* as Dante's self-conscious wish to give his contemporaries a new literary tradition of their own. Of course, for Dante there was no such thing as "Italy." The nation, and with it a unifying language, would appear only six centuries later—thanks in part to the efforts of Dante himself. But there was already in Dante's time a sense of what a unifying Italian culture could be, and the way to access it, for Dante and his fellow poets, was by writing in their own native tongue, the *volgare* (vernacular or dialect). To speak of Beatrice, for Dante, was to employ the same rhetoric of love used by the great Roman poets like Ovid and Horace. Beatrice was not only a muse; she was the herald of a new literary tradition.

Thus, with the above-quoted passage from chapter 25 of the *Vita Nuova*—at the heart of the book and just a few chapters before the death of Beatrice—we come to the crux of Dante's "little book": to express his endless love for Beatrice, bearer of blessings, while also imbuing his work with the prestige of literary history. To achieve such a goal was a tall order for any writer, especially one so young, and the Dante of the *Vita Nuova* often falls short of his mark in a work that can lapse into opacity and repetition. Yet the promise of this youthful text is as explosive as anything Dante ever wrote, as it draws us into enigmas as haunting now as they were when they first appeared. Nowhere is that mystery more powerful than when, soon after Dante's declaration of his cultural mission in chapter 25, the *Vita Nuova* painfully shifts gears into an essayistic mode that anticipates its final word on the role and reach of poetry.

5. TRANSFORMING GENRE

How desolate the mighty city seems! This mistress of peoples seems like she has become a widow. I was in the middle of drafting this canzone ["I've been so long ensnared by Love"] and had nearly finished it when the Lord of Justice called this most gracious one to glory under the protection of the sacred Queen Mary, whose name was held in the greatest reverence by the blessed Beatrice.[26]

Thus Dante writes in chapter 28 of the *Vita Nuova*, announcing what had seemed preordained from the start of the *libello*: the "most gracious one," the alternately delicate and hieratic Beatrice, would be taken from him, and from the world, before her time. An unknown cause claimed the life of Beatrice Portinari in 1290 at the age of twenty-four. Her death was, at first, just the passing of a "muse": one of those eminently interchangeable *donne*, ladies, who had inspired Dante to write the *Vita Nuova* in the first place and share his poetic comings and goings with Guido and friends. One need only recall a glorious poem like Cavalcanti's "Chi è questa che vèn," "Who is she coming," to grasp the fungible nature of the sweet new style muse, her core of inscrutability rendered here by Ezra Pound:

> *No one could ever tell the charm she hath*
> *For all the noble powers bend toward her*
> *She being beauty's godhead manifest.*
> *Our daring ne'er before held such high quest;*
> *But ye! There is not in you so much grace*
> *That we can understand her rightfully.*[27]

One is left to grasp at the identity of this woman, the poem's object of wonder. Is she Cavalcanti's muse in the *Vita Nuova*, Mona Vanna, or another of his passing loves? What is she like—is she a Dantesque lady "intelligent in love," a woman with Beatrice-like grace? We can answer none of these questions. All we can be sure of is that she was *not* the wife of Guido, who married the daughter of the formidable Ghibelline general Farinata degli Uberti, a memorable character from Dante's *Inferno* 10, for political reasons. Otherwise, the reader lingers in the terrain of unknowing and uncertainty that surrounds all of the sweet new style muses. Dante was certainly no feminist in our modern understanding of the term: from his earliest to his final work, the position of the male at the centers of power and nodes of privilege remained fixed. But what he did with regard to female identity in the *Commedia*—create a highly individuated Beatrice who speaks her mind, who can be bristling and even unpleasant (Borges acidly referred to her as a strident "bluestocking"[28])—was revolutionary. The seeds for his reconfiguration of the medieval muse were planted in his disorientation after the death of Beatrice, when the *Vita Nuova* transitions from its straightforward prosimetrum form into an essayistic mode.

Of course, the *Vita Nuova* is not an essay in our modern understanding of the term—that is, the genre of prose meditation and literary reflection on various topics, which did not fully emerge until the work of Renaissance pioneers like Michel de Montaigne and

after him Francis Bacon. The essaylike nature of the
Vita Nuova is more existential than rhetorical. At a key
moment in the narrative and because of a tragic event,
both the author and the protagonist, Dante, lose their
way and—in the spirit of the essay—the text attempts to
write its way toward a resolution in a winding, nonlinear
fashion that draws as much attention to its process as it
does to its conclusion.

After Beatrice's death is mentioned in chapter 28,
chapter 29 offers the strangest, most unsatisfying thoughts
in what had been shaping up to be a remarkable work:

> Let me say that, using Arabic numbers, Beatrice's
> noble spirit departed at the ninth hour of the ninth
> day of the month. According to the Syrian calendar,
> she left us in the ninth month of the year, their initial
> month being Tishrin the First, which is our October.
> According to our system, she died at that point in
> the Christian era AD when the perfect number had
> repeated nine times during her century: 1290. She
> was a thirteenth-century Christian.

The reader wants to shout, *No, Dante, no numerology,
not now!* Beatrice has died, the cataclysmic event has
rendered the city, by Dante's own accounts, "widowed,"
yet the poet insists on reverting to the stale and
unconvincing numerological patterns with which he
began the *Vita Nuova*. This move is especially unsettling
because, just chapters earlier, Dante had offered readers

a genuinely moving and frightening premonition of Beatrice's death, in a delirious dream-vision that found him visited by strange women with terrifying hair:

> In the beginning of these random thoughts, some disheveled women appeared to me and said, "You too will die." After these women, more strange and horrible-looking faces also appeared, adding, "You are dead."
>
> As my imagination wandered about like this, I came to a point where I no longer knew where I was. I seemed to see ladies passing on the street, with uncovered heads and crying furiously, looking extraordinarily sad. The sun seemed blotted out from the sky, as the stars themselves appeared to weep. I pictured dead birds falling from the heavens and tremendous earthquakes. Pondering these phantasms and feeling quite scared, I imagined a friend of mine saying to me, "Did you not know? Your miraculous lady has left this earth."

Earthquakes, premonitions of death, disturbing omens, birds falling from the sky: everything associated with Beatrice's passing is supercharged and overwhelming. So the bean counting with the number nine in the chapter following her actual death is beyond disappointing. Something seems to have snapped inside in Dante, unraveled in the narrative thread of the *Vita Nuova*. Dante the character is now looking for a new way of life, just as Dante the writer now seeks a new literary form. It will take several chapters of *errare*, the "error" or wandering mentioned in his dream of the disheveled women, to resolve both of these dilemmas. In this transition, which can be called an "essay" in the etymological sense of an attempt in literary form, the *Vita Nuova* goes from being a promising if uneven work with flashes of brilliance to a genuine masterpiece.

It would take Dante a full year, and six chapters (29–34), to navigate this change. On the one-year anniversary of Beatrice's death, the poet found himself in the center of the city, distracted, grieving, bathed in tears—and, of all things, drawing an angel:

> On the one-year anniversary of when our lady Beatrice was made citizen of the eternal life, I sat somewhere thinking of her and drawing an angel on some panels.[29] While I drew, I turned my eyes and saw that some distinguished men had gathered around me, watching what I was doing. From what they told me later, they had been watching me longer than I was aware. When I saw them, I got up to greet them and said, "Someone was with me just now, that's why I'm so pensive." After they left, I returned to my work, drawing these angelic figures.

The scene reveals the depth of Dante's grief. No interchangeable muse, no numerological pattern, could distract him from Beatrice's death. I believe that Dante never "loved" Beatrice in the conventional, sexual sense. The evidence overwhelmingly suggests that they met only a few times and had no physical contact.[30] Meanwhile, his "literary" love for her was typical of the sublimated version that sweet new style poets felt for their muses. But Beatrice's death changed all that. It was a genuine tragedy: a young, beautiful woman was called to the afterlife in the full flower of life, and the irruptive nature of this death sent Dante into a tailspin.

Dante's fellow poets in the sweet new style were probably none too pleased with his stubborn grief and inability to move on and find another muse. It is impossible to say whether Guido Cavalcanti's legendary rebuke of Dante was motivated by his friend's endless sorrow over Beatrice's passing. But whatever its inspiration, the language of Guido's "I' vegno il giorno a te infinite volte," "I visit you daily, and endlessly," clearly shows how little the "new" Dante—the one who emerges after Beatrice's death—had in common with the earlier Dante:

> *I visit you daily, and endlessly*
> *And you, forever, in base thoughts I find:*
> *It grieves me so that from your noble mind*
> *Much of the power is stripped it seems.*
> *Lightly scornful of many minds;*
> *Always fleeing the people's harm;*
> *Speaking of me so from the heart,*
> *I would welcome your every rhyme.*
> *Now I dare not, your life being so vile,*

Give any proof that your words please me
Nor come to you, that you might see me,
Yet if you read this sonnet frequently,
The evil spirit that pursues you closely
Summoned will vanish from your soul.[31]

As the harsh, accusatory verses suggest, the poetic break
between Dante and Guido was now complete. In chapter
34 of the *Vita Nuova*, we find a Dante who is unable to
move on, who cannot continue writing the *Vita Nuova*,
as he is symbolically stalled in the middle of Florence and
distractedly drawing an angel while paralyzed by grief.
This essayistic section of the *Vita Nuova* marks the tran-
sition from the death of Beatrice and the inert numer-
ology it had initially generated to an image of pure,
immobile grief, of such a pitch that it likely compelled
Dante's poetic mentor to call him to task for it. To picture
Dante drawing this angel is to imagine a narrative black
hole swallowing up the *Vita Nuova*, leaving the reader to
wonder if and how it would continue. Help was needed.
Thankfully, for Dante, it was about to arrive in the form
of what seemed to be a second Beatrice: a *donna gentile*,
gracious lady, with lovely, pitying eyes.

6. DISCOVERING "DANTE"

Had Dante followed the logic of Cavalcanti's sweet new
style poetics, the tragedy surrounding Beatrice's death
would have been a relatively brief one. No fellow poet

among Dante's *fedeli d'Amore* would have questioned the searing intensity of his grief. After all, the poetry of the sweet new style was laced with visceral motifs of suffering and anguish in the name of love—including one poem by Cavalcanti whose narrator is so wrecked by the effects of passion that his writing instruments must speak on his behalf.[32]

By the time he drew his angel, Dante's bereavement had gone on long enough to raise a poetic eyebrow. But all would have been forgiven had he followed the narrative logic of his own *Vita Nuova*—especially in chapter 35, when lightning seems to have struck the lovelorn poet twice:

> Soon [after my drawing of the angel], when I happened to find myself in a place that made me think of past times, I was feeling melancholic and filled with sad thoughts that gave me a frightful look. Aware of my terrible state, I lifted up my eyes to see if anyone could see me. Then I saw a very beautiful and gracious young lady, who was looking at me so compassionately from her window that all pity seemed concentrated in her.

The encounter is logical: a poet as soul-baring as the young Dante was bound to hear the call of passion once again, and a good amount of time had passed since Beatrice's death. The attraction on both sides was palpable, as later Dante would say that his "eyes started to take too much delight in seeing her." Despite her compassionate nature, this *donna gentile*—who would later resurface as the muse of his *Convivio* or *Banquet* of philosophical speculation—threatens the very structure and meaning of the *Vita Nuova*, and Dante knows it. He begins to curse his "wandering eyes," saying to them, "You used to draw tears from those who saw your sad state, and now it seems that you wish to forget it because of this lady who looks at you—yet she does so only out of mourning for that glorious Beatrice whom you too used to mourn." Amid this battle between love lost and love potentially regained, Dante has a vision: "there appeared inside me one day, close to the ninth hour of the day, a powerful image of the glorious Beatrice, dressed in that crimson dress she first wore before my eyes." From that point on, the *donna gentile* does not stand a chance. Dante chases away her temptations and pledges himself exclusively to Beatrice's ghost.

Ultimately, this embrace of Beatrice's love in all its spiritual purity did not bring immediate closure—nor did it lead to the discovery, in the *Vita Nuova* itself, of a new way of writing. For as Dante was forced to admit at the end of the book, Beatrice's majesty was such that he would be silent until he could speak of her in more worthy terms at some unspecified later date. But the text does signal that Dante's notion of the reader, and of his audience, has changed. In chapter 40, just after Dante's memory of Beatrice vanquishes the appeal of the gracious lady, the poet watches as some pilgrims pass through Florence on their way to Santiago de Compostela, where they will visit the grave of St. James the Great, an apostle of Christ. A thought comes to Dante—one that would change the course of his career, bring the *Vita Nuova* to its conclusion, and alter forever literary history:

> Thinking of them, I said to myself, "These pilgrims have apparently come from far away, and I do not believe that they have heard anything about Beatrice, about whom they know nothing. In fact, their thoughts are on other things, perhaps their faraway friends, whom we do not know." Then I thought, "I know that if they were from nearby, they would seem troubled because this city is now widowed. If I could capture their attention a bit, I would make them weep as they left the city, for I would write words that would bring tears to anyone's eyes."

For the first time in the book—and in Dante's life—he decides to write for an anonymous group removed from his restricted, lofty social world. For the first time, one could say, Dante is reaching out to the *generic reader*, anticipating the drive for universality that will make his *Commedia* a book for any and all who find themselves in the *selva oscura*, dark wood.[33] His need to communicate with the *peregrini pensosi*, pensive pilgrims, is Dante's way of saying farewell to his Dead Poets

Society and its aristocratic sweet new style. The symbolic break with Cavalcanti's poetics is thus complete, as the insecure, striving poet of the early chapters of the *Vita Nuova* matures into a writer dedicated to reaching the broad public. His soul forged in the smithy of grief, Dante discovered the version of himself that would one day be capable of writing a poem on the state of the human soul after death.

The *Vita Nuova* has always raised more questions than it can answer. So it seems fitting to end by hazarding an explanation for Dante's astonishing, unexpected turn away from the *donna gentile*, with her promise of more sweet new style love, and his move toward the anonymous readers represented by the pensive pilgrims of chapter 40. As I said, I do not think that Dante loved Beatrice in the sexual, romantic sense. But that does not mean that he did not love her as a person. I believe that the grief Dante narrates in those essayistic chapters after Beatrice's death is genuine and heartfelt: the young poet was encountering the cruel, unexpected death of a young woman he cared about, and the experience was debilitating. What the ancients called magnanimity, greatness of soul, found its expression—and enabled Dante to find his poetic calling—through his struggles with untimely death. He learned that muses, like people, are not interchangeable, and that the loss of a loved one can create a hole in the soul, just as it does in the narrative of the *Vita Nuova*. We are fortunate today that Dante's act of defiance in the face of this sorrow was to try to fill it with a new and revolutionary form of poetry, an expression in verse of his unshakable, unbreakable devotion, in her death, to the woman who had first brought his writing to life.

A NOTE ON THE TEXT

T HE *VITA NUOVA* has a complicated publication history, and scholars remain divided about its final form and chapter divisions as well as its actual title.[34] There is no original "autograph" version of the text directly attributable to Dante, and the earliest Tuscan manuscript copies—including two in Giovanni Boccaccio's illustrious hand—date back to the fourteenth century. The first printed edition of the *Vita Nuova* did not appear until 1576, making it one of the last of Dante's works to appear in print. This so-called *editio princeps* was not only late in coming: at least one copy was heavily censored by the Spanish Inquisition for what was deemed its inappropriate and heretical religious language, especially Dante's supposedly idolatrous depictions of Beatrice.[35] The initial complete English translation of the *Vita Nuova* was published as late as 1846 by Joseph Garrow, but then quickly forgotten because of Dante Gabriel Rossetti's groundbreaking translation soon after, in 1861.[36] Encouraged by his friend and fellow author Margaret Fuller, Ralph Waldo Emerson had translated the *Vita Nuova* in 1843, but the work remained unpublished until 1957.[37] The steady rise in interest in Dante since then, especially in academic circles, has witnessed the appearance of several new English translations of the once obscure *libello*.[38]

This translation of the *Vita Nuova* is based on the widely diffused and deeply influential critical edition by Michele Barbi, originally published in 1907 and then reissued in a revised and expanded form by Bemporad in 1921 and 1932 as well as Florence's Società Dantesca Italiana in 1960.[39]

VITA

NUOVA

1.

IN THE EARLY, nearly empty part of my Book of Memory there is a chapter with the Latin title "Here begins the new life."[40] I intend to copy into this little book the words I find written under it—if not all of them, at least their essence.[41]

2.

THE SUN had already circled the earth nine times since my birth when the glorious lady of my mind appeared before my eyes. Many called her Beatrice, she who blesses, even if they did not know her name. She had been in this world long enough for the heaven of the fixed stars to move a twelfth of a degree to the east.[42] So she was in the beginning of her ninth year when I saw her, while I was at the end of mine.[43] She was dressed in the noblest of colors, an understated and dignified crimson, with her clothes cut and adorned in a manner appropriate for her young age. I confess that at that point my animal spirit,[44] which dwells in the heart's most secret chamber, began to tremble so violently that I could feel its pain even in the farthest reaches of my blood. Trembling, the spirit said in Latin, "Here is a god stronger than I am, who comes to dominate me."[45] Then this awestruck animal spirit, which lives in the brain that receives the perceptions of all the other sensitive spirits, directed its words to the eyes and said to them in Latin, "Your bliss has now appeared."[46] My natural spirit, which is found in the part of us that controls our digestion, began to cry, and in tears it said in Latin, "Oh miserable me, what endless obstacles await!"[47]

From then on Love governed my soul, which surrendered to him entirely. He ruled over me with so much assurance and authority, fueled by my imagination, that all I could do was satisfy his every wish. He would order

me to seek out the young, angelic Beatrice, so in those
early years I often went searching for her and found her
looking so noble and praiseworthy that she recalled those
words of Homer: "She seemed the daughter not of a mor-
tal man, but of a god."[48] Even though Love ruled over
me through her omnipresent image, which was so pure
in essence that it never allowed him to guide me without
the sound advice of reason in those matters where it was
useful. Since it may seem absurd to go on speaking of
the passions and deeds of one so young, I will now stop.
I will also omit many other things that I could have cop-
ied from the source of these recollections in my Book of
Memory, and I will return to material written in more
important chapters.

3.

AFTER SO MUCH TIME had passed that it had been exactly nine years since the appearance of the gracious Beatrice, this miraculous woman once again appeared to me, dressed in the purest white and standing in between two older ladies. Crossing the street, she glanced toward where I stood agitated, and with her indescribable courtesy, which today is rewarded in heaven, she greeted me so virtuously that I felt as though I were witnessing the very limits of bliss. Her precious greeting reached me at precisely the ninth hour of daytime, three p.m. Since this was the first time her words reached my ears, I felt such rapture that I left the crowd of people like a drunk and took refuge in the familiar place of my own room,[49] where I began to think about this courteous one. Meanwhile, a gentle sleep overtook me, and I had a remarkable vision: a cloud the color of fire seemed to appear in my room, inside of which I saw the figure of a lord whose look would have frightened anyone who beheld him—yet he also appeared to be filled with a marvelous joy. He spoke many Latin words, but I understood little except for "I am your master."[50] I thought I saw a person sleeping in his arms, and she was nearly naked, wearing only what appeared to be a slight red slip. When I looked closely, I realized it was the woman of my salvation: the same Beatrice who had deigned to greet me the day before.

It looked like this figure, Love, was holding something burning in one of his hands, and I believe he said to me in Latin, "Behold your heart."[51] After some time passed, he seemed to unveil this sleeping woman and force her to eat the object burning in his hand—which she did fearfully. His joy soon turned to blackest sorrow. Weeping, he gathered the woman in his arms, and made as though he were rising heavenward with her. By then my light sleep could no longer bear the immense pain I was feeling: it broke and I awoke. I began to think things over, realizing that I had this vision in the fourth hour of the night, one a.m. So clearly it had occurred during the first hour of the last nine hours of nighttime.

Reflecting on what had I just seen, I decided to make it known to many of the famous poets of the time, since I was already familiar with the art of verse. I chose to write a sonnet addressed to all of Love's faithful,[52] describing what I had seen in my sleep and asking them to interpret my vision. So I began this sonnet that opens, "To every captive soul."

> To every captive soul and gentle heart,
> I now address these words of mine to you
> In hope you will return with a reply,
> As I salute our lord, the god of Love.
> A third of night already had eclipsed
> The shining of the brightest stars on high,
> When suddenly Love came before my eyes—
> The thought of him still haunts my troubled mind.
>   He held my heart in hand and seemed all joy,
> My sleeping lady wrapped inside his arms.

Then he awakened her and she, in fright,
Began to humbly eat my burning heart.
And then I saw him disappear in tears.

This sonnet is divided into two parts. The first offers greetings and asks for a reply. The second describes what the reply should be about and begins, "A third of night already had eclipsed." Many responded to this sonnet with different opinions.[53] Among those who answered was the one I call my best friend,[54] and he composed a sonnet that begins, "I think all virtue came before your eyes." Our friendship started when he learned that I was the one who had sent out the sonnet. The true meaning of my vision was not grasped by anyone at the time—but now it is clear to even the most simpleminded.

4.

AFTER THIS VISION, my natural spirit was soon blocked in its function because my soul was wholly consumed with thinking about the gracious Beatrice. So in a short while I became so frail and weak that many of my friends were worried about my frightful appearance. The more envious were already maneuvering to discover things about me that I wanted to hide at all costs. Aware of their wicked questioning—and following the wishes of Love, who had been wisely advising me—I answered that it was Love who had taken such control of me. I spoke of Love because I bore so many traces of him in my looks that my words were impossible to deny. When people asked me, "On whose account has Love ravaged you?" I merely smiled and looked at them without answering.

5.

ONE DAY the most gracious woman of all, Beatrice, was sitting in a place where prayers were being offered to the Queen of Glory, Mary, and I could see my bliss from where I stood. Directly between her and me, there was a refined lady of great beauty who looked at me several times, curious about my expression and thinking that it was meant for her. At that point, many became aware of her staring. I left soon after and heard people saying, "Notice how that woman destroys him." When they named her, I understood that they were speaking of the one who had stood directly in front of Beatrice when I was gazing at her. This comforted me, as I assured myself I had not revealed my secret love for Beatrice earlier that day with all my staring. I thought of making that other lovely woman a "screen" for the truth, and I succeeded so much in doing so that in a short time all those who spoke of me believed that they knew my secret. I admired this woman for months and even years, and to make the others believe in my ploy, I wrote some random poems for her that I have no intention of revealing here—except for when they relate to the gracious Beatrice. So I will leave them all out and include only what is in praise of her.

6.

I SHOULD ADD that this woman became so effective
a defense for my actual true love that I felt it was
necessary to record the name of the gracious Beatrice
and accompany it with those of other women, especially
the gentle screen lady's. I listed the names of the sixty
most beautiful women in the city where my Beatrice had
been placed by Almighty God, and wrote an epistolary
poem in the form of a Provençal "service song," which I
will not include here.[55] I would not have even mentioned
it, except to say that when I composed it, my Beatrice's
rank turned out miraculously to be none other than ninth
among the names of these women—as though she would
have it no other way.[56]

7.

THE SCREEN LADY whom I had used for so long to hide my true feelings had to leave our city and go to a distant place. I felt almost overwhelmed by the loss of this beautiful woman, becoming sadder than I would have imagined. I realized that if I did not speak with great pain about her departure, people would become aware that I had been disguising my feelings. I decided to turn my sorrow into a sonnet. I wrote it making sure that all, even the unsophisticated, would think that this screen lady had inspired my words. So I composed the sonnet that starts, "O you who ride the road of Love."

> *O you who ride the road of Love,*
> *Please look and ask yourself if there*
> *Exists a pain as grave as mine.*
> *I only ask that you might deign*
> *To hear me speak and then decide*
> *If I am not grief's home and host.*
> *Not for my little worth but through*
> *Its noble ways, the lord of Love*
> *Once gave to me a life so sweet*
> *And smooth, that often it was said:*
> *"O God, what virtues make this man*
> *Have such a lightness in his heart?"*
> *   No longer bold, I've lost the strength*
> *That issued from abundant love.*
> *I'm now reduced to loss so great*

That I've no heart to write a verse.
I am indeed like those who wish
To hide the shame of all they lack,
And so put on a look of joy.

This sonnet has two main parts. In the first, I intend to summon Love's faithful with those words of the prophet Jeremiah, "O all you who pass me by, come and see if there is a suffering equal to mine."[57] In the second, I describe the condition Love reduced me to, which differs from my state in the last part of the sonnet, where I tell of what I have lost. The second part begins, "Not for my little worth."

8.

AFTER THIS LOVELY screen woman left, it pleased the Lord of all angels to call to His glory a very attractive young lady, renowned for her grace in our city. I saw her body at final rest attended by many women, all of whom were crying out of immense pity. Remembering that I had seen the departed in the company of the most blessed Beatrice, I could not hold back my own tears. Weeping, I decided to say some words about her death, a tribute for having sometimes seen her with my lady—a point that I make in the last part of the poem, as will be quite clear to anyone with common sense. So I wrote these two sonnets, the first beginning, "O weep, lovers," and the second, "O wretched death."

> *O weep, lovers, as Love now weeps,*
> *As you learn why his tears abound.*
> *Love hears his ladies cry in pain,*
> *With bitter grief upon their eyes,*
> *Since wretched Death has cruelly wrought*
> *His vicious ways in gentle hearts,*
> *Destroying all the world can praise*
> *In a gentle lady—just virtue lives.*
> > *Now hear how Love so honors her:*
> *I saw him spilling human tears,*
> *Gazing upon her lifeless form.*
> *He often looked up to the sky,*

Where this lady's soul now resides,
She who once was a joy to see.

This initial sonnet is divided into three parts. The first summons and begs Love's faithful to weep and tell them that their lord is crying, as I write "As you learn why his tears abound" to get them to listen to me. The second describes the reason for these tears, and the third discusses the honors that Love bestowed upon this deceased lady. The second part begins, "Love hears," and the third, "Now hear."

  O wretched Death, no pity there,
You mother of most ancient woe,
Severe and grave in all you judge,
Since you have filled my heart with grief
As I walk down the path of pain,
My tongue will always curse your name.
And if I wish to see you beg for peace,
It's clear that I must speak of crimes,
Of guilt you bear in every guilty thing,
And not because your nature is unknown,
But rather to enrage all those
Who always feed on hopes of love.
  You've always wanted to destroy
The grace that wins a woman's praise:
While she was still a youthful girl,
You crushed the lightness[58] of her love.

Don't wait for me to say her name,
Her qualities all make it plain.
The one who merits no such grace
Can never hope to share her space.

This sonnet is divided into four parts. The first calls Death by some of his proper names, and the second, speaking of Death, explains why I felt like cursing him. The third goes on the attack and the fourth speaks to the wider public, so that they can grasp my meaning. The second part begins, "Since you have filled," the third, "And if I wish," and the fourth, "The one who merits no such grace."

9.

SOON AFTER the death of this young woman, some-
thing came up that made me leave our city and travel
toward where my screen lady was living, although my
final destination was not as distant. Though I was with
many fellow travelers, it was clear that the journey so
displeased me that my sighs[59] could barely relieve the
anguish in my heart over having to separate myself from
my bliss. Then sweet Love, who ruled over me through
the agency of the gracious Beatrice, appeared to me in
the form of a pilgrim humbly dressed in rags. He seemed
bewildered,[60] staring at the ground continuously except
for when his eyes apparently turn toward a beautiful
river, swift and translucent, that flowed along the road I
was traveling. I sensed Love calling out to me, saying, "I
come from that woman who was your screen for a long
time, and I know that she will not be returning to your
city anytime soon. So I have with me the heart that you
once gave to her, and I will give it to a new woman who
will act as your shield, just as that other lady had." He
named her, and I knew her well. "But if you should repeat
of any of these words I have said to you," Love contin-
ued, "do so in a way that will not reveal the falseness
of the love you bore for that first woman, and now must
show for another." Having said these words, his vision
vanished from my mind, where it seemed that Love had
given so large a part of himself. Looking like a different
person, I rode that day deep in thought and filled with

sighs. Afterward I described this episode in a sonnet that begins, "Some while ago I rode a path."[61]

> *Some while ago I rode a path,*
> *In bitter thoughts about my trip,*
> *When I met Love along the way,*
> *In clothes that humble pilgrims wear.*
> *He seemed a shell of his old self,*
> *Devoid of all his past renown.*
> *He moved toward me with thoughtful sighs*
> *And lowered head, averted gaze.*
>   *When he saw me, he called my name,*
> *And said, "I come from distant parts,*
> *Where by my will your heart once lived,*
> *And now must serve a new delight."*
> *Then I absorbed so much of him*
> *That he was gone, I know not how.*

This sonnet has three parts. The first describes how I found Love and what he looked like. The second says what he told me, though not all of it, for fear of revealing my secret. The third narrates how he disappeared. The second part begins, "When he saw me," and the third, "Then I absorbed so much."

10.

AFTER MY RETURN, I began to look for this new woman whom Love had named on the road of sighs, and to be brief, I will say that I soon made such a screen of her that many people began to speak of the situation in less than polite ways, which had me quite worried. For this reason—that is, because of the vicious rumors that were damaging my reputation—the gracious Beatrice, enemy of all vice and friend of all virtue, passed me on the street and denied me her sweet greeting,[62] where all my bliss resided. Now I must depart a bit from my present story to explain the powerful effect her greeting had on me.

11.

I MUST SAY that whenever Beatrice appeared some-
where, the prospect of her miraculous greeting would
render it impossible for me to make an enemy, as it
would fill me with a flame of charity that compelled me
to pardon anyone who might have offended me. If any-
one asked me what was happening at times like these, I
would simply answer, with a look of humility, "Love."
When she was about to greet me, one of Love's spirits,
destroying all the other senses, would drive the weak
spirits out of my sight and say to them, "Go and honor
this lady of yours," and Love would take their place.
Anyone who wished to know Love could have done so
by looking at the trembling of my eyes. When the gra-
cious Beatrice greeted me, not even Love was power-
ful enough to lessen my unbearable bliss. Instead, and
as though he were possessed by an excess of sweetness,
Love became so overwhelming that my body, which by
then was entirely under his control, would move like
a heavy, inanimate thing. So it was clear that my bliss
resided in her greeting, which often surpassed and over-
whelmed my faculties.

12.

Now, returning to our story, let me say that once the bliss of her greeting was denied to me, I fell into such pain that I went off alone to bathe the ground with the bitterest tears. After my weeping had relented a bit, I returned to my room, where I could cry without being heard. Begging my gracious lady for mercy and saying, "Love, help your faithful one," I fell asleep there, crying like a beaten child. About halfway through my sleep, I seemed to see—near me in my room—a young man dressed in clothes of the purest white. He was apparently deep in thought and staring at me where I lay. After looking at me for some time, I heard him call out to me in sighs, with these Latin words: "My son, the time has come to set aside our lies."[63] I recognized him as the one who had visited me in my dreams many times before. As I stared at him, he appeared to be weeping in pity and waiting for my answer. Composing myself, I began to speak to him and asked, "Master of all that is worthy, why are you crying?" He answered me in Latin, "I am like the center of a circle with equidistant points—but you are not."[64]

Thinking over his words, I felt he was talking in riddles, so I forced myself to answer him in this way: "My lord, why do you speak to me so mysteriously?" He responded in Tuscan, "Do not ask for more than what is useful." But I began to talk with him about the greeting that had been denied me, and I asked him for the reason. He said, "That Beatrice of ours heard some people talking about you, saying how you offended the screen woman whom I had mentioned to you on the road of sighs. So our gracious one, who is the enemy of all strife, did not deign to greet you, since you had been so obnoxious. And since Beatrice has actually known the gist of your long-held secret for quite a while, I would like you to write some verses that describe the power that I, Love, have over you because of her, and how you have devoted yourself to her ever since you were a boy. Call as your witness he who knows all this, and ask him to speak to her—then I, who am that witness, will gladly explain everything to her. This way, she will understand your true motive, and with this knowledge she will be able to grasp the meaning of those words of yours that have deceived others."

Love continued: "Let this poetry you write act as an intermediary, so you will not be speaking directly to her, which would be inappropriate. Do not send your words anywhere she might hear them unaccompanied by me. And make sure to adorn them with sweet music, which I will accompany them with when necessary." Having said these words, Love disappeared and my sleep was broken. I remember having this vision during the ninth hour of daytime. Before leaving my room, I decided to write a ballad that would follow what my lord had proposed to me. So I composed one that begins, "I want you, ballad, to find Love."

I want you, ballad, to find Love,
And to my lady go with him,
So that he makes this plea you sing
The cause that frees me from my guilt.
　　So graceful, ballad, are your ways,
That you can go alone and free
To anywhere you wish to be.
But if you want to rest assured,
You must first find the lord of Love,
To not do so would be unwise.
Since she whose words you must receive
Is likely angry toward me now—
And if you're not accompanied by me
She's bound to hold you in contempt.
　　When Love's beside you then you'll start
To sing with these sweet-sounding words,
But only after she forgives.
"My lady, he who sends me here,
Asks you to hear with open heart,
And then decide if he's to blame.
I come with Love, your beauty's liege,
Who can destroy your lover's looks.
See how his eyes were led astray
By Love—but not his steadfast heart."
　　Tell her, "My lady, he whose heart
Has been of such firm faith to you,
That serving you is his sole aim.
He has been yours and never strayed."

If she does not believe your words,
Send her to Love, who knows the truth:
And end by praying on bent knee,
That if her pardon can't be had,
Then she can send me to my death,
And I will gladly heed her wish.

    Before you go away from me,
Tell Love, who's pity's truest friend,
And who knows how to plead your case:
"By way of my melodic notes,
Remain here at our lady's side,
Say what you will about this man,
And if your case should win her grace,
Then let her smile[65] announce this peace."
O gentle ballad, when you like,
Go sing to her where honor lives.

This ballad is divided into three parts. In the first, I tell it where to go, and comfort it so that it can go safely.[66] I tell it what company to keep if it wishes to go securely and without any danger. In the second, I say what the ballad wishes to make clear. In the third, I give it permission to go forth as it wishes, commending its journey to the arms of fortune. The second part begins, "When Love's beside you," and the third, "O gentle ballad."

I could be accused of not knowing to whom I am addressing these words in the second person, since the ballad is nothing more than I myself speaking. I will answer by saying that I intend to resolve this issue in an even more difficult part of this little book—anyone who doubts my practice here, and in that later section, will find their objection addressed there.

13.

AFTER THIS VISION I have just described, when I had already written the words that Love had asked me to, I began to be assailed and tempted by many disparate thoughts, against which I was quite defenseless. Among them there were four that seemed to trouble me the most. One was that the rule of Love is good when he removes all evil things from the mind of his faithful servant. The other was that Love's dominion is not good when the pain and suffering of this faithful servant increase in proportion to his devotion. Another was that the name Love is so pleasing to hear that it seems impossible for it to have anything other than a sweet effect, for names tend to be like their referent—as the Latin phrase goes, "The name derives from the thing itself."[67] Finally, I realized that the lady who had so enthralled me was not like women in general, whose feelings can be quite fickle. These thoughts were so disorienting that I felt like someone who does not know which way to turn, and who wants to move but does not know where to go. The only way I could find common ground in these thoughts and unify them was extremely unpleasant to me, for it would have meant appealing to Lady Pity and hurling myself in her arms. Languishing in this state, I felt like writing some poems. So I composed the sonnet that begins, "My thoughts all tend to speak."

My thoughts all tend to speak of Love,
And are of such a varied kind,
That one believes Love rules as friend,
Another calls his power crazed,
Another brings me hope and joy,
Another makes a flood of tears.
The goal of pity's all they share,
Quaking with fear that fills my heart.
So I don't know which theme to choose,
And though I wish to speak, words fail.
I find myself ensnared by Love!
The only harmony of mind
Can come from one whose help I loathe,
That Lady Pity who's my shield.

This sonnet is divided into four parts. The first states and proposes how all my thoughts are about Love. The second says they are different and describes why, and the third indicates what they all have in common. The fourth part narrates how, in my wish to speak to Love, I do not know which theme to choose—and that, if I were to find the one way to harmonize my thoughts, I should name my enemy, Lady Pity. I call her "Lady" in an almost disdainful way. The second part begins, "And are of such a varied kind," the third, "The goal of pity's all they share," and the fourth, "So I don't know."

14.

AFTER THE WAR of these conflicting thoughts,[68] the gracious Beatrice happened to turn up where many other gentle ladies had gathered. A friend of mine had brought me there thinking it would give me pleasure, as this was a spot where many women were parading their great beauty. Not actually aware of where I was being led, and trusting in the friend who had brought me to what was in fact the point of death, I said to him, "Why have we come to these women?" He answered, "To make sure they are well served."

The truth is that these women were there to join a lady who had just been married that day. According to the customs of our city, they had to accompany her at the first meal she served in the home of her new spouse. Thinking I was doing my friend a favor, I decided to attend to the women keeping her company. As soon as I made my decision, I seemed to feel an intense tremor arise in the left side of my breast[69] that spread immediately through the rest of my body. Fearing that someone had noticed my trembling, I confess that I simultaneously leaned against a painting that ran along the walls of the house and, opening my eyes to look at the women, found the gracious Beatrice among them.

My spirits were so destroyed by the force of Love when I found myself beside this blessed lady that only my spirits of vision remained alive,[70] even though they were outside of their usual place because Love had taken over their proud home in order to behold the miraculous lady. As debilitated as I was, I pitied those little spirits,[71] which were complaining bitterly and saying, "If Love had not blasted us like lightning from our spot, we could have stayed and beheld the wonder of this lady as so many of our companions do." Now many of the women present, noticing my transformation, began to be amazed. Talking among themselves, they mocked[72] me to the gracious Beatrice. At that point, my friend, whose mistake in taking me to these women had been made in good faith, took me by the hand and dragged me out of their sight, asking me what was wrong. After resting a bit—and with my dead spirits revived and my displaced ones restored to their proper place—I replied, "I have just set foot in that part of life beyond which one cannot go and hope to return." After leaving my friend, I returned to my bedroom of tears, where, weeping in shame, I said to myself, "If this Beatrice knew my condition, I do not think she would mock me. In fact, I think she would feel great pity for me." Amid these tears, I decided to write some words that would address her and explain the reason for my transformation, since I was well aware that it was unknown—and that, if it were known, I think it would elicit pity from all. So I wrote the sonnet that begins, "You and your ladies."

You and your ladies mock my ways,
But you do not consider why
I seem so strange to all of you

When I behold your gorgeous form.
If you knew why I act like this,
Pity herself would call a truce.
For Love, when he finds me with you,
Becomes assured and quite adept
In laying low spirits that fear,
Destroying here, displacing there,
Leaving only the sight of you.
Then I become another man,
Yet not so much that I still can't
Hear cries of spirits lost in pain.

I do not divide this sonnet, since that is done only to reveal the meaning of the individual parts. Since its meaning should be quite clear, it has no need of division. It is true that even in those sections where the meaning of this sonnet is self-evident, there are some mysterious words, like when I say that Love killed all my spirits, and that the visual spirits alone remained alive, except that they were outside of their usual place. Such enigmas are impossible to fathom for anyone who is not among Love's faithful. Those who are of this group will easily understand the apparent mystery. But it is not right for me to clarify it, for in so doing my words would be either useless or unnecessary.

15.

AFTER THIS strange transformation of mine, an intense thought came and stuck with me and indeed continued to haunt me: "Since you are reduced to such a miserable state every time you see this lady Beatrice, why do you continue to seek her out? What if she were to ask you that question now, what would you answer her—assuming that you were even physically capable of doing so?" Another thought rose in humble reply to that one: "If I were not to lose my faculties, and if I were free enough to answer her, I would tell her that the moment I call to mind her miraculous beauty, I am so overcome by the desire to see her that it kills and destroys anything in my memory that might arise against this wish—and that my past sufferings do not hold me back from trying to see her." Moved by such thoughts, I decided to write some words that would excuse me from that earlier misgiving, and that would explain what happens to me when I am in her presence. I wrote the sonnet that begins, "Whatever might keep me away."

> *Whatever might keep me away*
> *Dies when I see you, gorgeous joy,*
> *And when you're near I feel the Love*
> *Who says, "O run, escape from death."*
> *My face shows that color of heart,*
> *That's close to death and seeking help—*
> *Trembling just like a drunken man,*

The stones appear to cry, "Die! Die!"
    He sins who sees my soul bewitched[73]
And offers me no aid, when all
He needs to do is share my pain
In pity, which your mocking killed,
After my eyes brought it to life,
When all they sought was death's release.

This sonnet is divided into two parts. In the first, I say why I do not keep away from this woman, Beatrice. In the second, I say what happens when I go near her. That part begins, "And when you're near." This second part is divided in five sections, based on five narrative points. In the first, I say what Love, moved by reason, tells me when I am near her. The second describes how the state of my heart is expressed in my face, and the third relates how all my confidence abandons me. The fourth claims it would be a sin not to comfort me, and that showing pity would be the way to do so. The last part describes why others should pity me because of the pathetic sight that I offer. But that pitiable sight goes unnoticed, since it was destroyed by the mockery of our Beatrice, who led others—those women who might have noticed my pitiable sight—to follow her in making fun of me. The second part begins, "My face shows." The third, "Trembling just like a drunken man," and the fourth, "He sins." The final section starts, "In pity."

16.

AFTER WHAT I SAID in this sonnet, I felt the need to write more so that I could mention the following four things about my condition that I did not believe I had yet made clear. First, I felt pained many times when my memory pushed my imagination to describe what Love was doing to me. Second, Love often assaulted me so suddenly and completely that nothing of me remained alive except for a thought that spoke of this lady, Beatrice. Third, when this battle of Love ravaged me to such a degree, I moved about almost drained of color as I sought out this woman, believing that the sight of her would defend me in my struggle, and forgetting what actually happened to me when I got close to such graciousness. Finally, seeing Beatrice not only failed to defend me, but ultimately destroyed what little life was left in me. So I wrote the sonnet that begins, "So many times."

> *So many times there comes to mind*
> *Confusing thoughts that Love creates,*
> *And so much pity swallows me—*
> *Alas, do others feel it too?*
> *For Love's attack is so complete*
> *My life almost abandons me,*
> *One lone spirit remains alive,*
> *Enduring just to speak of you.*
> *I force myself to push ahead,*
> *And barely living, without strength,*

I come to you, hoping for health:
And if I raise my eyes to see,
A tremor starts within my heart,
Which makes the soul depart my blood.

I divide this sonnet into four parts to tell four stories. Since they are described above, I will only say how each begins: the second starts, "For Love's attack," the third, "I force myself," and the fourth, "And if I raise."

17.

AFTER WRITING these three sonnets addressed to Beatrice—all of which leave little unsaid about my condition—I thought I would remain silent and say no more because it seemed that I had made everything clear. Yet though I no longer addressed her, I felt the need to gather new and more lofty material than in the past. Since the reason for this new material is pleasing to hear, I will describe it as briefly as I can.

18.

MY APPEARANCE gave away my heart's secret to many people. Some women, who well understood my heart because they had seen me faint on different occasions, had gathered to enjoy one another's company when I passed by them, as if sent by fate. One of these ladies, who had a lovely way of speaking, called to me. When I stood before them, I noticed that my most gracious Beatrice was not among them. Thus assured, I greeted them and asked how I could be of service. The women's group was large in number, and some of them were laughing among themselves. Others were looking at me, waiting for me to speak. Others conversed among themselves. One of them turned her eyes to me and called me by name, asking, "Why do you love this woman, since you cannot bear to be in her presence? Tell us, since certainly the goal of such a love must be rather unusual."

After saying these words to me, she and all the other women waited for my reply, which was "Ladies, the goal of my love was to be greeted by the woman that you may be referring to. In that greeting lay my bliss and the aim of all my desires—but since she has decided to deny it, Love, in all his mercy, has placed my bliss in something that cannot be denied to me." The women began to speak among themselves, and as we sometimes see rainfall mixed with snow, I thought I heard their words mixed with sighs. After they had talked, the one who had initially addressed me said, "We beg you to tell us where this bliss of yours resides." I answered, "In those words that praise my lady." That same woman replied, "If you are telling the truth, then those words that you just told us describing your condition must have meant something else." Thinking over her words, I left the ladies in shame and began to say to myself, "Since there are so many words that can praise my lady, why have I ever written in any other way?" So I decided to make the praise of Beatrice the subject of my writing. But thinking this over, I felt I was taking on a theme too lofty for me, one that made me afraid to begin. So I lingered for many days in this state of wanting to write, but in fear of beginning.

19.

THEN ONE DAY as I walked along a long path that went along a limpid stream, I suddenly felt the need to write a poem and began to think about how I would go about it. I felt that I should not speak of Beatrice unless I addressed my words to ladies—and not just any ladies but only those who are gracious and not run-of-the-mill. Then my tongue began to speak as if moved by itself, uttering the words "Ladies who are intelligent in love." I kept these words in my mind with great joy, thinking that I would use them as my beginning. After returning to our city, and reflecting for some days, I began a new canzone[74] with that opening line and structured it in the way you will see below. The canzone begins, "Ladies who are intelligent in love."

> *Ladies who are intelligent in love,*
> *I wish to speak of my woman to you,*
> *Not thinking that I can exhaust my praise,*
> *But rather to relieve my troubled mind.*
> *I say that when I speak about her worth,*
> *Love makes me feel a sweetness so complete,*
> *That if I managed not to lose my strength,*
> *I would inspire that same love in all.*
> *And I wish not to speak in such high terms*
> *That if I fail I would appear quite base.*
> *But I will speak of her surpassing grace*
> *In humble words that are unfit for her,*

For only you, ladies and maids in love,
Are apt for such a lofty theme as this.
    An angel calls out to the Lord above
And says: "O God, a marvel lives on earth,
A soul whose splendor reaches up to us."
And heaven high, whose only fault is this,
That she's not there, now asks its Lord for her,
And all the saints cry out for mercy's gift.
Just Lady Pity stands behind our cause,
For God replies, about this cherished one,
"O my belovèd ones, suffer in peace,
For she, your hope, abides down here below,
Where there is one who fears her loss of life,
And who will tell to all the damned in hell,
'O cursèd ones, I have seen hope so blessed.'"
    The lady is desired up above:
I wish to tell you now about her worth.
I say, whoever wants to be with grace,
Should go to her, for when she walks about
Love sends a chill into the wicked heart,[75]
So that their thoughts are petrified and die.
And he who tries to stay and gaze at her
Will feel ennobled or instead will die.
And when she finds someone who may deserve
To gaze at her and feel all of her force—
Indeed it happens that she gives to him
Humility as well as her goodwill,
So that he must forget every offense.
She has received such grace from God above,

That whoever speaks of her can't but win.
      Love says of her, "She's but a mortal thing—
How can she be so beautiful and pure?"
He looks again and tells himself it's true,
That God has wished to make a form so new.
She almost has an alabaster hue,
As apt for one with such a humble soul:
The gifts of nature live inside of her.
In her alone lies beauty's highest truth.
And from her eyes as she moves them about,
Come burning spirits filled with flames of love,
Destroying any eyes beholding them,
And penetrate until they find the heart.
You all see Love's imprint upon her face,
There where nobody can direct their gaze.

      I know, canzone, that you'll go around
Speaking to ladies when I send you forth.
I warn you now, because you've been to me
A child of Love, so innocent and young,
Please ask of anyone whose path you cross:
"Direct me to my place, for I've been sent
To find her in whose praise I am now dressed."
And if you want your path to be unblocked,
Do not remain among the base and low;
Try, if you can, to be a pleasing song
To ladies and to men imbued with grace,
Who will send you upon the quickest path.
You will find Love within their rank and file,
Speak well of me to him as duty bids.

To make it understood, I will divide this canzone more finely than my other works. I first separate it into three parts. The first functions as an introduction, and the second considers the main theme. The third basically glosses what precedes it. The second begins, "An angel calls out," and the third, "I know, canzone." The first part is divided into four sections: in the first, I say to whom I wish to speak about my lady, and why. In the second, I describe what it feels like when I think of her qualities, and how I would write if my nerve did not fail me. In the third, I mention how I plan to write about her in order to avoid succumbing to cowardice. In the fourth, addressing once more my chosen audience, I say why I am speaking to them. The second begins, "I say," the third, "And I wish not to speak," and the fourth, "For only you, ladies and maids."

When I write, "An angel calls," I begin to describe our Beatrice, dividing this section in two, the first depicting how heaven is aware of this lady, and the second how the earth is as well—all of this comes after the line "The lady is desired." This second part is divided in two, the first is on the nobility of her soul and all the impactful powers that issue from it, the second on the nobility of her body and beauty, described in the lines beginning, "Love says of her."

Starting at "And from her eyes," this second part is divided in two. The first tells of the beauty that everyone finds in Beatrice, and the second her specific beauties. The next section is also divided in two. In the first, I write about her eyes, which are the source of love. In the second, I speak of her mouth, which is the supreme object of my passion. In order to dispel any vile thought, the reader should understand that Beatrice's greeting, which issues from the mouth, was the goal of all my longing as long as I was able to receive it. When writing, "I know, canzone," I add a stanza almost as a coda to the others, describing what I desire from this poem of mine. Since this last part is easy to understand, I will not bother with more analysis. I will say that, to open up the meaning of this canzone to more people, it would be necessary to break it into even smaller units. But if someone is not smart enough to understand the sections as I have them above, I would not mind for him to leave me be. For I feel I have communicated to too many the meaning of how these different parts of the poem were made—if it should happen that anyone would even bother to heed them.

20.

AFTER THIS CANZONE became rather well known among the public,[76] one of my friends heard it and felt compelled to ask me to tell him who Love was. Apparently my words had given him a higher opinion of me than I deserved. Because of my earlier treatment of the theme of ladies intelligent in love—and because I felt I owed it to my friend—I thought it would be good to try to do the same for Love, so I decided to write some words on this subject. Hence my sonnet that begins, "Love and the gentle heart."[77]

> *Love and the gentle heart are one,*
> *As wrote the great poetic sage,[78]*
> *Such that dividing them would be*
> *Like having sense devoid of soul.*
> *Loving nature creates the two,*
> *With Love as lord, the heart his home,*
> *Inside of which he sleeps in peace,*
> *Sometimes a bit, sometimes for long.*
> *   A lady's beauty then appears,*
> *To please the eyes and fire the heart*
> *To long for such a lovely thing—*
> *At times it lasts there for so long*
> *That it awakes the soul of love,*
> *As ladies are by valiant men.*

This sonnet is divided into two parts. In the first, I describe how much potential resides in Love. In the second, I say how much of that potential can be translated into action. The initial part is divided in two sections: the first depicts the spirit where this potential resides, and the second how this spirit and potential come into being, one relating to the other as matter does to form. The second begins, "Loving nature creates." When I write, "A lady's beauty then appears," I am describing how this potential translates into action and is initially realized in a man—and in a woman as well, when I write, "As ladies are by valiant men."

21.

AFTER DISCUSSING LOVE in the previous poem, I also felt like writing words in praise of this most gracious Beatrice that would show not only how she awakens Love from where he sleeps, but also how she miraculously makes him appear in places where he is unlikely to be found. So I wrote the sonnet beginning, "My lady brings love to the eyes."

> *My lady brings love to the eyes,*
> *To see her is to feel her grace.*
> *All men stare where she passes by,[79]*
> *Her greeting causes trembling heart,*
> *So that, eyes down, a man turns pale,*
> *Lamenting over his defects,*
> *As she dispels all pride and wrath.*
> *O ladies, help me sing her praise.*
>   *Things sweet and of a humble form*
> *Are born in hearts who hear her speak—*
> *Praised be the first who sees her grace.*
> *Her look when she begins to smile*
> *Cannot be cast in words or thought,[80]*
> *So rare is her celestial gift.*

This sonnet has three parts. The first describes how this lady transformed the potential of Love into action through the magnificence of her eyes, and the third how this transpired through her glorious smile. In between these parts, there is a very small one that is almost like a beggar with respect to the other two, and it begins, "O ladies, help me." The third part begins, "Things sweet and of a humble form."

The first part is divided in three. The first tells of how she powerfully imbues grace into everything she sees. This is a way of describing how she brings Love into action even where he does not exist. The second depicts how she transforms Love into action in the heart of all those who see her. The third tells of the virtue she instills in their hearts. The second begins, "To see her," and the third, "All men stare." When I say, "O ladies, help me," I am addressing those who can help me praise Beatrice. When I write, "Things sweet," I am repeating what I said in the first part, but here as it relates to two actions of her mouth: one, the sweetness of her words, and the other, her miraculous smile. But I do not describe how this smile of hers works in the hearts of others, for human memory cannot fully comprehend either that smile or its effects.

22.

NOT LONG AFTERWARD, and as pleased the great Lord who Himself accepted death, the man who had been the father of so wondrous a creature as Beatrice departed from this life and certainly went on to eternal glory.[81] This loss was a cause of great pain to those who lived on and were his friends. Since there is no friendship more intimate than that of a good parent to his good child and vice versa—and since both Beatrice and, as many believed, her father were good to the highest degree—she was thus obviously filled with the bitterest pain. In such sad cases, it was the custom of our city that women and men associated with the dead would gather separately. Many ladies came to Beatrice as she wept her piteous tears. I saw them returning from her and heard them describe her grief, with words like "Certainly she is weeping so much that whoever sees her would die from pity."

Other women passed by, and I was overcome by such sorrow that my face was bathed in tears and I had to use my hand to cover my eyes. I would have hidden myself as the weeping assailed me, if it were not for the fact that I was in the very spot where many ladies were coming from Beatrice, and I wanted to hear what they said about her. So I stayed put as they passed me by, saying, "Who among us could be happy, since we have heard that lady speak so piteously?" After this some other women passed by as well, adding, "This man weeps exactly as though he has seen her, just as we have." Others said of me, "Look how changed this man is, he no longer seems himself!"

Thus did I hear those women speak of Beatrice and me in passing. Afterward I thought about it and, since I had such a worthy theme, I decided to write a poem that would include everything the women had said. Since I would have gladly questioned them had it not seemed inappropriate, I wrote as though I were actually asking them questions and they were answering. I composed two sonnets: the first asks the questions I had in mind, while the other gives the answers, reporting what I actually heard the ladies say and using that as their reply. I begin the first, "O you who go with humble looks," and the other, "Are you the one who often has described."

> *O you who go with humble looks,*
> *And lowered eyes, expressing pain,*
> *Where do you come from that your face*
> *Has turned to white in pity's hue?*
> *Perhaps you've seen our lady's face*
> *Awash in gentle tears of Love?*
> *Reveal, ladies, what's in my heart,*
> *For all that's base is foe to you.*
>
> *If you come from a scene of grief,*
> *Please stay and rest with me a bit,*
> *And do not hide her state from me.*
> *I see your eyes filled up with tears,*

And see you coming back so changed,
It breaks my heart to find you thus.

This sonnet is divided into two parts. The first calls upon and asks these ladies if they are coming from Beatrice—and tells them that I believe this to be the case, since they are returning looking so ennobled. The second begs them to speak of her and begins, "If you come."

Here is the sonnet I wrote afterward, as I mentioned before.

Are you the one who often has
Described our lady, just to us?
Your voice seems to resemble him,
Your figure though seems someone else.
Why do your tears come out in floods?
Bringing pity to all who see?
Did you witness her tears and then
Fall prey yourself to savage grief?
Let us endure the pain and tears
(To comfort us would be a sin),
For we have heard her voice through tears.
She shows such pity in her face
That who may dare to look at her
Might die from weeping while they stare.

This sonnet has four parts, to give the ladies whom I address four ways of speaking. Since it is quite clear from the sonnet, I will not explain the meaning of its parts, and will only indicate where they start. The second begins, "Why do your tears," the third, "Let us endure the pain," and the fourth, "She shows such pity."

23.

A FEW DAYS AFTERWARD, a painful ailment began
to afflict me, so that for nine days I continued to suffer
bitter pain, which reduced me to such weakness that I
had to stay put like an invalid. On the ninth day, as I felt
a nearly intolerable pain inside, a thought of my lady
Beatrice came to me. As I reflected for a while about her
and my incapacitated state—and realized how short life
is, even when one is healthy—I began to cry inside about
all this misery. Sighing heavily, I said to myself, "One
day the gracious Beatrice will certainly die." I was so
troubled that I closed my eyes and fell into an agitated
delirium that sent my mind racing. In the beginning
of these random thoughts, some disheveled women
appeared to me and said, "You too will die." After these
women, more strange and horrible-looking faces also
appeared, adding, "You are dead."

As my imagination wandered about like this, I came
to a point where I no longer knew where I was. I seemed
to see ladies passing on the street, with uncovered heads
and crying furiously, looking extraordinarily sad. The
sun seemed blotted out from the sky, as the stars them-
selves appeared to weep. I pictured dead birds fall-
ing from the heavens and tremendous earthquakes.
Pondering these phantasms and feeling quite scared,
I imagined a friend of mine saying to me, "Did you
not know? Your miraculous lady has left this earth." I
began to weep from pity, not only in my imagination

but also with my eyes, bathing myself in actual tears. I imagined looking heavenward and thought I saw a multitude of angels returning above, trailing before themselves a gentle white cloud. These angels appeared to be singing gloriously, and I could make out some of their Latin words, "Hosanna in the highest!"[82] The rest I could not hear.

My heart, which was bursting with love, seemed to say, "It is true: our lady lies dead." Because of this I apparently went back and sought out the body that held our most noble and blessed Beatrice, and my wild fantasy was so intense that it revealed this lady as dead. Other women were apparently covering her head with a white veil. Her face seemed to carry a look of such pity that it said to me, "I now see the source of all peace."

Because of this image I so humbly wished to see her that I called to Death and said, "Sweet Death, come to me, and do not be cruel. You should instead be kind, considering where you have been! Now come to me, for I greatly desire you—as you see that I do, since I wear your pallor." When I saw all the sad rituals for the bodies of the departed completed, I imagined that I had returned to my room and turned toward heaven. My imagination was so strong that, weeping, I began to say in a truthful voice, "O beautiful soul of Beatrice, how blessed is he who beholds you!" As I uttered this grievous gush of words and summoned Death to come to me, a young and gracious lady who was alongside my bed—and who thought that my tears and words were a result of my illness—began to weep in great fear. Other ladies in the room became aware that I was crying because of her tears. After sending away this woman, who was one of my closest relations,[83] they came toward me to awaken me, saying, "Sleep no more," and "Do not be afraid."

At these words of theirs my wild fantasies ceased, just as I was on the point of saying, "O Beatrice, how blessed you are," and after having already said, "O Beatrice." I opened my eyes and saw that I was mistaken. As much as I tried to call out this name, my voice was so broken by the pain of weeping that I believe these ladies could no longer understand me. As ashamed as I was, I was prompted by Love to look their way. When they saw me, they began to say, "He seems dead." Then they said to one another, "Let's try to comfort him." This prompted many words of consolation from them, as they even asked me what had frightened me. Somewhat comforted, and realizing that I had seen only false images devoid of reality, I replied, "I will tell you what happened." I recounted to them what I had just seen from start to finish, without naming that most gracious one.

Healed of my illness, I decided to write about this experience, believing it could be moving to hear. So I wrote the canzone "A humble lady, young in years," which is clearly organized into the parts I will describe below.

A humble lady, young in years,
Adorned with many gentle ways,
Was where I often called to Death—

She saw the pity in my eyes,
And listened to my empty words.
So moved was she with fears and tears,
That other ladies by my side
Asked her to leave the place we were,
Then they approached me with these words.
Some said, "You must no longer sleep,"
Others, "Why are you so afraid?"
And so I left my vivid dreams,
While calling out my lady's name.

    My voice was so replete with pain,
And broken up by force of woe,
That only my heart heard her name.
And as my face was filled with shame,
Which covered me from high to low,
Love placed me in my ladies' way.
My aspect made them so amazed,
That they could only speak of death.
"Oh let us bring comfort to him,"
They humbly said among themselves.
"What did you see that stole your strength?"
They asked, and after I was calm,
I said, "O ladies, I'll relate."

    As I thought on my fragile life,
And saw how fleeting is its length,
Inside my heart, his home, Love spoke,
All sighs as he expressed his thoughts.
"Of course, my lady too must die."
These words brought me such heavy grief,

And so I shut my wounded eyes,
With spirits so riven with pain
They fled and fainted all alone.
Continuing my wild dream,
From truth and reason rent apart,
I saw the women's angry looks,
And heard them say, "You'll die, you'll die."
  Then I saw such disturbing things
In this strange space I now was in
Without knowing just where I was.
Apparently there passed by me
Some ladies with disheveled hair,
Some weeping, others filled with wails,
Their woes like arrows dipped in flame.
And then I seemed to see the sun
Turn black—a star appeared, and both
The sun and star began to weep.[84]
The birds above fell to the ground,
And earth below did tremble so.
A man appeared all pale and weak,
And said to me, "What's happened here?
But don't you know the latest news?
Your lady once so fair lies dead."
  I raised my eyes replete with tears,
And saw, as though a gift divine,
The angels flying up above,
A little cloud before them all,
Sounds of "Hosanna" filled their cries—
That's all I can report to you.

Lord Love then said, "I hide no more:
Now come to see your lady's rest."
My wild fantasy conveyed
Me to my lady's sad remains,
And when I found her body there,
I saw her face covered by veil,
She wore a look of modest grace,
As if to say, "I am in peace."
    So humble did my pain make me,
Seeing her in this humbled state,
That I could say to Death, "I hold
You dear, and gentle you must be,
Since you've been by my lady's side,
And so have pity not disdain.
You see my yearning so intense
To be with you, that we're alike.
O come, accede to my heart's plea."
Sad rites complete, I took my leave,
And when I was alone, I raised
My eyes to heaven high and said,
"O blessed who sees your lovely soul,
You who in mercy just called me."

This sonnet has two parts. In the first, speaking to an unidentified person, I describe how I was roused from a wild dream by some ladies, and how I promised them I would write about it. In the second, I write what I said to them. The second begins, "As I thought on my fragile life." The first part is divided in two: the first describes how these women—one in particular—responded to my dream when I returned to my normal state, and the second how they told me to abandon my delirium. This part begins, "My voice was so replete." When I write, "As I thought on my fragile life," I am describing my vision to them. This section contains two parts. The first is all about my vision, and the second tells of the time they called to me, and how I thanked them discreetly. That second part begins, "You who in mercy."

24.

AFTER THIS WILD FANTASY, one day as I was sitting somewhere deep in thought, I began to feel a tremor in my heart, as though I were in the presence of my lady Beatrice. A vision of Love appeared to me, and he seemed to be coming from the place where my lady was, and it was as though he said to my heart, "Remember to bless the day that I took hold of you, it is no less than your duty." This certainly thrilled my heart—so much so that it felt like it was no longer my own. A bit later, as my heart spoke to me with Love's words, I saw a gracious lady coming toward me, one renowned for her beauty. She was the love of my best friend.[85]

Her name was Giovanna, but because she was so beautiful some called her Primavera, or Spring. This became her alias. Looking behind her, I saw the miraculous Beatrice approaching. These women passed me by, one after the other, and it seemed as though Love were speaking these words in my heart, "That first one is called Primavera only because of how she came today, which is why I inspired the creator of her name to call her thus, for she will be the 'first to arrive' [*prima verrà*] on the day that Beatrice reveals herself afterward in a dream to you, her faithful one. And if you really think about her name Giovanna, you will realize that it means 'she who will come first,' since it derives from Giovanni Battista, John the Baptist, who came before the True Light and said, 'I am a voice crying out in the wilderness—prepare yourself for the way of the Lord.' "[86]

After these words, I also seemed to hear Love say, "If you think about the matter clearly, Beatrice should be called Love, since she resembles him so closely." Thinking things over, I decided to write to my best friend—without mentioning certain words it seemed tactful to pass over—because I believed his heart still held a place for this gracious Primavera. So I wrote the sonnet that begins, "I felt awaken in my heart."

> *I felt awaken in my heart*
> *A spirit that had been asleep.*
> *And then I saw approaching Love,*
> *So joyful that his look was new.*
> *He said, "Now think how best to honor me."*
> *His laughter filled all of his words.*
> *As I stood thus beside my lord,*
> *I looked to see from whence he came,*
> > *While Vanna and Bice approached*
> *Together to right where I stood,*
> *Two wonders in a single line.*
> *As memory recalls it now,*
> *Love said to me, "That one is Spring,*
> *The other Love, since she's like me."*

This sonnet has many parts. The first tells how I began to feel a tremor awaken in my heart, and how Love seemed happy there as I beheld him at a distance. The second describes how Love seemed to speak in my heart, and the third how he had stayed with me in this happy state before I saw and heard certain things. The third part begins, "As I stood thus," and it is divided in two, the first section devoted to what I say and the second to what I hear. That second section begins, "Love said to me."

25.

AT THIS POINT any person worthy of having their doubts cleared up might be wondering whether I am speaking of Love as though he were an actual being—that is, not just an intellectual substance, but rather a physical body. Yet such a concern would be based on a false assumption. For Love is not an entity unto itself, as is the case with all substances; rather, it is an accident within a substance.[87]

I speak of Love as though he had a body and were a man in three ways. I describe my seeing him "approaching" because it connotes forward motion and the intrinsic capacity for movement, which according to the Philosopher, Aristotle, is a unique property of corporeal entities—so clearly I am proposing that Love has a body. I also say that he "laughs" and "speaks," which seem to be human properties, especially the capacity for humor. So it is obvious that I am personifying Love.

To clarify this matter in a suitable way for the present, one must first understand that in the past there were no poets who wrote of love in our Tuscan dialect or vernacular.[88] Instead, poets who wrote of love did so in Latin. Among us Italians, as likely happens among other peoples—for example, the Greeks—it was the more traditionally literary poets (that is, those who favored Latin) and not the vernacular ones who wrote of love. It was not long ago that those first vernacular poets appeared. I believe that, to a certain degree, to write poetry in the vernacular is no different from writing it in Latin. To get a sense of just how brief the history of vernacular poetry is, you will not find a Provençal or Italian poem written more than 150 years ago. This is the reason a few poetic hacks gained renown, simply because they were the first to write in the dialect.

The first poet who felt the need to write in the vernacular did so because he wanted his words to be understood by women who had great difficulty with Latin. This practice goes against that of poets who write on matters other than love—which is why vernacular poetry came into being in the first place. Since greater license was given to poets than to prose writers, and since these poets were mostly writing in the vernacular, it is natural and just that they were granted more freedom than other writers who were also using the dialect. After all, if some figure of speech or other rhetorical touch is granted to the Latin poet, it should also be to the vernacular one as well.

So if Latin poets were free to speak of inanimate objects as though they had sense or reason, and even allowed them to address one another—and if they did this not only with real things but also with invented ones (that is, they spoke of things that do not exist and yet that have the capacity for speech, and they gave voice to many accidents, as though they had substance or were human)—then vernacular poets should also be able to do the same, but not without some good reason that they could then later explain in prose.[89] That poets have written like this is clear from such examples as Virgil, when he says that Juno, the enemy of Troy, speaks to Aeolus, Lord of the Winds, in the first book of the *Aeneid*, "Aeolus, only to you."[90] To which he replied, "It is for you, Queen, to command, and for me to obey."[91] This same poet speaks of things that are animate and inanimate in book 3 of the *Aeneid*, writing, "Long-suffering sons of Dardanus."[92] Lucan also personifies animate and inanimate objects, writing, "Rome, you still have gained from the civil wars."[93] In Horace's *Art of Poetry*, one man speaks to his own inspiration as though it were another person—not so much in Horace's own words but rather by echoing Homer: "Speak to me, Muse, of the man."[94] Ovid writes of Love as though it were human in the beginning of his *Remedies for Love*, "It is war for me, I see, war for me."[95] All this is clear to anyone who doubts my little book. To make sure that no uncouth person takes issues with my words, I will add that just as the Latin poets could not write without justification, so too must vernacular ones have cause for what they say. So it would be a shame for any poet to dare say things with personification and rhetorical figures and then, if asked to remove this verbal dressing and reveal his poem's essence, find himself unable to explain himself. My best friend and I know exactly who these foolish versifiers are.

26.

THIS MOST GRACIOUS BEATRICE, about whom I just spoke in the preceding poems, brought so much glory to people that when she passed them by, they would run to see her. This made me marvelously happy. When somebody was with her, so much honesty would come to that person's heart that he would not dare to raise his eyes, nor respond to your greeting. The many who experienced this can verify it for those who do not believe it. Crowned and clothed in all modesty, she would circulate without partaking of any of the glory that she saw and heard.

After she passed by them, many would say, "This is not a lady—she is more like one of the beautiful angels in heaven." Others said, "She is a miracle, blessed be the Lord who works in such miraculous ways!" I must say that she showed herself to be so gracious and charming that those who beheld her would feel a pure and sweet delight, so great that they would be unable to describe it. Then there were others who would begin to sigh the moment they gazed at her.[96] These are some of the remarkable effects that she so powerfully set in motion. Remembering all this, and wishing to praise her, I decided to write some words about her marvelous and brilliant qualities, so that she might be known to not only those who could see her in person, but also those encountering my words. So I wrote the sonnet that begins, "So gentle."

So gentle and so pure appears
My lady to all those she greets,
That every tongue would tremble, mute,
And no eyes dare to turn her way.
She moves about, followed by praise,
Benignly dressed in modest ways,
And seems a thing come down to earth,
A miracle from heaven high.
     She seems so pleasing to our sight,
That eyes give gladness to the heart,
A feeling that we can't explain.
It also seems her lips give birth
To sweet spirits replete with love,
Who whisper "Sigh" inside the soul.

Based on what I have recounted earlier, this sonnet is so clear that it has no need of division. So let us leave it at that. At this point my lady Beatrice had become so beloved that not only was she honored and praised, but so were the other women who associated with her. Seeing this, and wanting to make it clear to those who did not, I decided to write a poem about it. So I composed this other sonnet that begins, "He sees virtue revealed," which describes how her power worked in others, as is clear from the poem's structure.

He sees virtue revealed, that sees
My lady with her women friends.
All those who go with her are moved

To thank God for his gift of grace.
Her beauty is so great a force,
That none can stoop to jealous acts,
Instead they hope to be like her,
With love, and faith, gentle thoughts.
        The sight of her spreads humble ways—
Not only does her beauty shine,
But all near her share in her praise.
So gracious are her acts, that none
Can bring them back into the mind,
Except in sighs of sweetest love.

This sonnet has three parts. The first describes the people to whom this lady seemed especially remarkable, and the second how gracious her company was. The third is about her powerful effects on others. The second part begins, "All those who go with her," and the third, "Her beauty is so great a force." This last part is divided in three. The first narrates what she brought to her fellow ladies—and that was known only to them. The second tells of what others observed happening to them. The third describes how she had these miraculous effects not only on women, but in all people—and not just when they were in her presence, but also when they recalled her in memory. The second begins, "The sight of her," and the third, "So gracious are her acts."

27.

AFTERWARD I BEGAN one day to reflect on what I had written about my lady in these two preceding sonnets. Realizing that I had not yet described her impact on me, it seemed to me that I had spoken insufficiently of her. So I decided to write some words about these effects and how she inspired virtue in me. Since I did not think I could do so briefly in a sonnet, I began a canzone that starts, "I've been so long."

> *I've been so long ensnared by Love*
> *And acclimated to his rule,*
> *That though I once found him so harsh,*
> *He's now all tender in my heart.*
> *But when he takes my force away,*
> *My spirits fleeing here and there,*
> *I feel my weakened soul turned sweet,*
> *My face emptied of all its hue.*
> *It's then I feel how Love controls,*
> *As all my spirits whirl and speak,*
> *And gushing forth and calling out*
> *My lady's name to make me whole.*
> *This always happens through her gaze—*
> *A humble thing beyond belief.*

28.

HOW DESOLATE the mighty city seems! This mistress of peoples seems like she has become a widow.[97] I was in the middle of drafting this canzone and had nearly finished it when the Lord of Justice called this most gracious one to glory under the protection of the sacred Queen Mary, whose name was held in the greatest reverence by the blessed Beatrice. Though some may want me to describe her death, I have no intention of doing so for three reasons. First, it is not part of my present plan, if we go back to the opening of this little book. Second, if it were part of the plan, my language would be insufficient to this task. Last, even if the first two reasons did not exist, it would not be right for me to describe her passing, for doing so would entail praising myself, which is highly inappropriate. So I will leave this task to some other commentator. Besides, since the number nine has played such a large role throughout our narrative, it seems appropriate to speak of her loss in reference to that number. So I will first describe the role it played in her death, then assign it explanations, showing why this number was so dear to her.

29.

LET ME SAY THAT, using Arabic numbers, Beatrice's noble spirit departed at the ninth hour of the ninth day of the month.[98] According to the Syrian calendar, she left us in the ninth month of the year, their initial month being Tishrin the First, which is our October. According to our system, she died at that point in the Christian era AD when the perfect number had repeated nine times during her century: 1290. She was a thirteenth-century Christian.[99]

The reason this number was such a friend to her could be this: according to both Ptolemy and Christian truth, there are nine moving heavens, and according to accepted astrological opinion, these nine heavens influence the world below in relation to their effects on one another. This number was special to her because in her age all nine planets of the Primum Mobile moved in perfect sync.[100] That is one way to consider it—but if you think about it more carefully, and in the light of incontrovertible truth, Beatrice was the number nine incarnate, so similar were they in my understanding. Three is the root of nine, as three times three is obviously nine. So if three is the root of nine, and if the root of all miracles is three—that is, the Father, the Son, and the Holy Spirit, who are three in one—then she was so closely aligned with the number nine that she was its living embodiment, that is, a miracle, whose root is none other than the miraculous Trinity. Perhaps a more subtle thinker would find a more subtle reason. But this is what I believe is true and find most appealing.

30.

AFTER SHE LEFT THIS WORLD, our city became like a widow stripped of all dignity. Weeping endlessly in this desolate city, I wrote to its leaders describing its condition, opening with the words of the prophet Jeremiah, "How desolate the mighty city seems." I mention this quote so no one will wonder why I included it earlier,[101] for it is meant to introduce the new material that follows it. If anyone wishes to reprimand me for not including the rest of my letter, I excuse myself on the grounds that my intent from the start has been only to write in the vernacular. Since all of that letter's words are in Latin, it would be outside of my aim to include them here. I know that my best friend, and this book's dedicatee, shares this view that I should write only in the dialect.

31.

AFTER MY EYES had wept for a while—and when they were so weary they could no longer vent my pain—I thought of unburdening myself with some sorrowful words. So I decided to write a canzone in which, while in tears, I spoke of Beatrice and all the suffering that was destroying my soul. I began with these words, "My sad eyes that pity the heart." To make this poem seem all the more widowed at its conclusion, I will explain it before you read it and from now on this will be my practice.

This sorrowful little song has three parts. The first is its proem, the second describes my lady, and in the third I speak to the canzone itself in all my sorrow. The second part begins, "Beatrice is in heaven high," and the third, "My sad canzone." The initial part has three divisions. The first explains why I decided to write, and the second indicates whom I am addressing. The third describes what I want to say. The second division begins, "Since I recall," and the third, "I will write." When I write, "Beatrice is in heaven high," I am referring to two parts of the poem: one tells why she was taken from us, the other how others weep over her loss. This section begins, "The beauty of her body gone," and is divided in three: the first describes those who do not weep for her, the second those that do, and the third my own condition. The third begins, "The deepest sighs." When I write, "My sad canzone," I am addressing the poem itself, commending it to certain women and bidding it to stay with them.

> *My sad eyes that pity the heart*
> *Are victims of so many tears,*
> *That now they are in full defeat.*
> *If now I wish to vent my pain,*
> *Which brings me close to death's own door,*
> *I must express my inner woe.*
> *Since I recall my joy to speak*
> *With you of my lady in life,*
> *O gentle ladies, you alone,*
> *And no other will hear these words.*
> *I will write of her through my tears,[102]*
> *For she ascended all at once,*
> *And left Love languishing with me.*
>   *Beatrice is in heaven high,*
> *The realm where angels find their peace—*
> *She left you, ladies, and joined them.*
> *No fire nor ice took her from us*
> *As they often with others do,*
> *Only her mercy made her go.*
> *The light of her most humble ways*
> *Attracted God Himself to her,*
> *His sweet longing for all she was*
> *Moved Him to call her blessèd soul*
> *To come to Him from here below—*
> *He knew that this, our tainted life,*

Could never suit that gentle one.
        The beauty of her body gone,
So full of grace her gentle soul,
She glories now in her true home.
Who weeps not when he speaks of her
Has heart of stone so cruel and vile[103]
That nothing good can enter there.
There is not in the lowly heart
The intellect to grasp her worth,
Nor is there will to weep for her.
And yet for those who can recall
All that our lady once had been,
And how she was taken away,
Then grief afflicts as does the need
For sighs and death by flood of tears—
And thus the soul's denied all hope.

        The deepest sighs can give me grief
When thoughts come to my tired mind
Of her who caused my heart's divide,
And often as I ponder death,
So sweet a wish for it arrives
It drains the color from my face.[104]
And when this image comes to me
Such pain afflicts my many parts,
Infusing me with bursts of pain.
Reduced I am to such a state
That shame divides me from the crowd.
In tears, alone in my lament,
I call to Beatrice and say—

In need to vent my pain—"You're dead?"
         In tears, torments, and anguished sighs,
My heart's destroyed and all alone,
A source of woe to all who hear.
No tongue could give account of what
My life became the moment when
My lady left this world of ours.
And so, my ladies, though I try,
I can't describe what I've become.
So sad has vile life made me,
Debasement now my only state,
And men who see my deathly face
All seem to say, "Away with you!"
But the true me one lady sees,
As I hope for the grace she grants.
         My sad canzone, go in tears,
And look for ladies and for maids
To whom your sister poems were sent
To signal the approach of joy.
And you, the daughter of despair,
Go sorrowful and stay with them.

32.

AFTER HAVING WRITTEN this canzone, there came
to me one who, in terms of my affection, was second only
to my best friend.[105] This man was closer in blood to our
gracious Beatrice than any other. While we were speak-
ing, he asked me to write a poem for him about a lady
who had died—but to pretend that I was writing about
another lady who was also dead. Realizing that he was
referring to our blessed Beatrice, I told him I would do as
he had bid me. After thinking the matter over, I decided
to write a sonnet that would express my grief, but make
it seem as though he had written it. So I wrote the son-
net that begins, "O come and listen to my sighs." It has
two parts, the first calls upon Love's faithful to listen to
me. The second describes my miserable condition and
begins, "The bleakest sufferings."

> O come and listen to my sighs,
> As pity wills, you gentle hearts.
> The bleakest sufferings recede
> And should they not I'd die of grief.
> My eyes have been so cruel to me,
> More often than I would have liked,
> With tears spilt in my lady's name,
> To vent the heart, which cries for her.
> You often hear my sighs invoke
> This gentle lady gone to dwell
> Up where her virtue now belongs—

In such contempt they hold this life
As if they were a doleful soul
Abandoned by the hope to heal.

33.

AFTER I WROTE this sonnet, I thought about the person on whose behalf I had composed it as though it were his, and I realized that my effort may have been weak and unconvincing for one as closely connected to our glorious Beatrice as he was. So before giving him the sonnet, I wrote two stanzas of a canzone—one truly on behalf of my friend, the other for myself, although anyone who considers them carefully will see that they come from the same source. The attentive reader will also see that different people speak in them, for one of them does not refer to Beatrice as "my lady," while the other clearly does. I gave him both the canzone and the sonnet, telling him I wrote it all for him.

The canzone begins, "How many times," and has two parts. In the first stanza of one of them, my good friend and this close relation of Beatrice laments. In the second, I myself grieve in the stanza that begins, "Then all these sighs of mine can blend." So it seems that in this canzone two people are suffering, one of whom grieves like a brother, the other like love's servant.

> *How many times, alas, I think*
> *That I will never see again*
> *My lady, so I go with grief,*
> *And so much pain inside my heart,*
> *That my afflicted mind cries out,*
> *"O soul of mine, why don't you leave?*

For torments such as you endure
On earth are of so dark a pitch
That they fill me with fearful thoughts."
Then I call out for Death,
As sweet and soft a form of rest,
And say, "O come," with so much love
That I seem jealous of the dead.
      Then all these sighs of mine can blend
Into a single searching sound
That always calls for Death—
For he has been my one sole aim
Since that lady of mine was robbed
From us by his savage decree.
Time was, her beauty shed such joy—
And now it's fled the eyes for good,
Transformed to loveliness of soul,
Sending to heaven up above
A light of love that angels see,
Causing their lofty minds to stare
In wonder at such female grace.

34.

ON THE ONE-YEAR ANNIVERSARY of when our
lady Beatrice was made citizen of the eternal life, I sat
somewhere thinking of her and drawing an angel on
some panels.[106] While I drew, I turned my eyes and
saw that some distinguished men had gathered around
me, watching what I was doing. From what they told
me later, they had been watching me longer than I was
aware. When I saw them, I got up to greet them and
said, "Someone was with me just now, that's why I'm so
pensive." After they left, I returned to my work, drawing
these angelic figures. As I did, I had the idea of writing
some poetry, in the form of an anniversary poem, for the
men who had just come to me. So I wrote this sonnet,
which has two beginnings. I will explain the poem with
regard to each of them.

Under the first opening, this sonnet has three parts:
the first describes how this woman was already in my
memory, the second tells what Love was doing to me,
and the third narrates his effects. The second begins,
"Then Love," and the third, "And tears departed." This
last part is divided in two, with the first describing how
all my sighs came out speaking, and the second how
some spoke differently from one another. The second
begins, "But those."

I divide the second opening in a similar way, except
that in the first part I describe when Beatrice first entered
my memory, which I do not do in the other.

First beginning

> *There came into my mind*
> *A gentle one who for her worth*
> *Was placed by highest God*
> *In humble realms where Mary reigns.*

Second beginning

> *There came into my mind*
> *A gentle one who makes Love weep,*
> *Just at the time when all her worth*
> *Brought you to see me as I drew.*
> *Then Love, who felt her in his mind,*[107]
> *Was roused from his own savaged heart,*
> *And told the sighs, "Get out of here."*
> *So that each one left in lament.*

> *And tears departed from my heart,*
> *With wails, they all left from my breast,*
> *In one sole voice that often sends*
> *The tears of woe to my sad eyes.*
> *But those that came with greatest pain*
> *Arrived to say: "O noble mind,*
> *A year has passed since your ascent."*

35.

SOON AFTERWARD, when I happened to find myself in a place that made me think of past times, I was feeling melancholic and filled with sad thoughts that gave me a frightful look. Aware of my terrible state, I lifted up my eyes to see if anyone could see me. Then I saw a very beautiful and gracious young lady,[108] who was looking at me so compassionately from her window that all pity seemed concentrated in her. Just as those who are suffering are moved to tears when they watch someone pity them, so too did my eyes feel the need for tears. Not wishing to show my weakness, I fled from the eyes of this gracious one, saying to myself: "There could only be in that lady the most noble kind of love." I decided to write a sonnet, in which I spoke to her, and which would narrate all that I have been describing. Since its meaning is quite clear, I will not divide it. The sonnet begins, "My eyes beheld."

> *My eyes beheld how pity's trove*
> *Was gathered in your face,*
> *When you saw how I looked*
> *And what I'd done in all my grief.*
> *Then I realized that you could grasp*
> *How sad my life had now become—*
> *At this my heart increased its fear*
> *That my eyes showed my lowly state.*
>   *And so I fled from you, and sensed*

The tears moving inside my heart,
Which thrilled in looking at your face.
I said to my benighted soul:
"That lady must be pledged to Love,
Who makes me go about in tears."

36.

IT TURNED OUT that whenever this woman saw me her face would take on a look of compassion and a pale color that suggested love—which often reminded me of the noble Beatrice, who also wore this hue. Unable to weep away or vent my sorrow, I often went to see this gentle lady, who seemed to draw the tears from my eyes with her gaze. So I felt the need to write some words addressed to her and composed this sonnet, which begins, "Color of love." Its content is clear and needs no explanation.

> *Color of love and pity's guise*
> *Have never with such wonder filled*
> *A lady's look as she espies*
> *Some gentle eyes or painful tears,*
> *As they came to your face when you*
> *Beheld the anguish writ on me.*
> *To see you thus brings to my mind*
> *A thought that could destroy my heart.*
> *I cannot keep my ruined eyes*
> *From staring at you without end,*
> *So greatly do they yearn to weep—*
> *And you increase in them that wish,*
> *Such that they only think to cry—*
> *And yet you cancel out all tears.*

37.

I BEGAN to go to see this woman so often that my eyes started to take too much delight in seeing her. The situation made me heartsick and filled with self-loathing. I often cursed my wandering eyes and said to them in my thoughts, "You used to draw tears from those who saw your sad state, and now it seems that you wish to forget it because of this lady who looks at you—yet she does so only out of mourning for that glorious Beatrice whom you too used to mourn. Do as you like, cursed eyes, but I will remind you that, until death comes, you should have never ceased to weep."

After I said this to my eyes, my sighs assailed me powerfully and painfully. To make sure this inner battle was known not just to me, the miserable man experiencing it, I decided to write a sonnet and express this horrible condition. So I wrote the sonnet that begins, "The bitter tears." It has two parts: in the first, I speak to my eyes as though I were talking to my own heart, and the second removes any confusion by showing who it is that speaks this way. This latter part begins, "So says." I could go on explaining, but it is unnecessary, for the preceding account makes my meaning quite clear.

> "*The bitter tears that you once shed,*
> *O eyes of mine, for such a time,*
> *Brought tears to eyes of others too*
> *For pity's sake, as you have seen.*

And now it seems you would forget,
If I should fail my mortal chore
Of recalling her at every turn,
The lady whom you once had mourned.
      Your faithlessness weighs on my thoughts
And frightens me, so that I dread
The face of her who looks your way.
You should never, until you die,
Forget your lady, who is dead."
So says my heart, and then it sighs.

38.

WHENEVER I RETURNED to see this new lady, the sight of her had such a strange effect on me that I often thought of her as someone who pleased me too much. "This is a gracious, beautiful, and intelligent young woman," I told myself, "who may have been sent by Love to bring peace to your life." I would think of her in even more loving terms—which pleased my heart greatly.

When I surrendered to this feeling, my reason asserted itself, and I said to myself, "God, what kind of thought is this, that tries to console me in such a vile way and keeps my mind from basically all else?" Then another thought arose in me, saying, "You have been through such a trial, why not remove yourself from that bitterness? You are witnessing Love's inspiration,[109] which immerses us in the desires of passion, and which has been set in motion in such a gentle way by the eyes of a woman who has shown you much compassion." Struggling within myself in this way, I wanted to write some words—and because the thoughts that spoke on this new woman's behalf were winning this internal battle, it seemed best to address them. So I wrote this sonnet that begins, "A gentle thought." I say "gentle" to describe the lady I am discussing, for in all other aspects the thought was quite vile.

In this sonnet, I divide myself into two parts, just as my thoughts were riven in two. One part I call "heart,"

that is, appetite. The other I call "soul," that is, reason. I
describe how one speaks to the other. It makes sense to
call the appetite "heart," as will be clear to those readers
I hope to reach. It is true that in the preceding sonnet I
take the part of the heart against the eyes, which seems
to contradict what I am saying at present. But here when
I say "appetite" I mean heart, which is to say that my
overriding wish was to remember that gracious Beatrice
of mine instead of gazing at this new woman—though
I did have some desire for her then, but it was faint. So
these two ways of speaking are not contradictory.

This sonnet has three parts: the first describes this
new lady and how all my desire bends toward her, and
the second tells of what the soul, or reason, says to the
heart, or appetite. The third gives its response. The
second part begins, "The soul says," and the third, "The
heart responds."

> *A gentle thought that speaks of you*
> *Comes often to reside in me,*
> *And talks of love[110] with words so sweet,*
> *The heart cannot fail to accede.*
> *The soul says to the heart, "Who's this,*
> *Who comes to set our mind at peace,*
> *Possessing powers so immense,*
> *That they would drive all thoughts away?"*
>   *The heart responds, "O thoughtful soul,*
> *This is a new spirit of love,*
> *Who brings all yearning on to me,*

And all its life and many strengths
Have come from eyes so pity bound
Because of our unceasing pain."

39.

AGAINST THIS ADVERSARY of reason there appeared inside me one day, close to the ninth hour of the day, a powerful image of the glorious Beatrice, dressed in that crimson dress she first wore before my eyes. She seemed to be as youthful as she was when she first came to me. So I began to think of her, and in these reflections about our past, my heart began to feel remorse over the base desire to which it had so long and vilely surrendered itself, against all reason. Distancing themselves from this vicious desire, all my thoughts turned to the gracious Beatrice. I should say that from then on I began to think of her so intensely with all of my shameful heart that my sighs were often proof of it. As they issued forth, they spoke the name of this most gracious one, and how she left us. Some of these thoughts were often so painful that I forgot what I was thinking and where I was.

This reemergence of sighs caused my pent-up tears to begin flowing again, making it seem that my eyes were two things whose sole wish was to weep. These long bouts of crying would bring a purple color to my eyes, a sign of the suffering they were enduring. So it seems they were justly punished for their wandering, and from that point on they could not look upon another who might return their gaze and elicit a similar effect. Wishing the death of this evil desire and vain temptation—and wanting to clear up any confusion about my earlier poetry—I decided to write a sonnet about what I have just described. So I wrote, "Alas! The full force of my sighs," with the word "alas" revealing my shame over how my eyes had wandered.

This sonnet needs no division, as its meaning is quite clear.

> *Alas! The full force of my sighs,*
> *All born from thoughts within my heart,*
> *Has brought defeat to my own eyes,*
> *Which dare not look at those who stare.*
> *They have become symbols supreme*
> *Of weeping and expressing pain,*
> *And often crying such that Love*
> *Encircles them with bitter crowns.*

> *These thoughts and sighs that I emit*
> *Become so anguished in the heart*
> *That Love faints from the strife endured.*
> *My lady's name is there to see,*
> *Inscribed upon these thoughts and sighs,*
> *With many words about her death.*

40.

AFTER THIS STRUGGLE, and during the time when many people went to see the blessed image that Jesus left us of His beautiful face—which my Beatrice now sees in all its glory—many pilgrims were winding their way through that city where our blessed lady was born and had died. These pilgrims were moving along, it seemed to me, deep in thought. Thinking of them, I said to myself, "These pilgrims have apparently come from far away, and I do not believe that they have heard anything about Beatrice, about whom they know nothing. In fact, their thoughts are on other things, perhaps their faraway friends, whom we do not know." Then I thought, "I know that if they were from nearby, they would seem troubled because this city is now widowed. If I could capture their attention a bit, I would make them weep as they left the city, for I would write words that would bring tears to anyone's eyes."

After the pilgrims passed out of view, I decided to write a sonnet expressing these thoughts. To make it more moving, I addressed the poem to them directly and wrote the sonnet beginning, "O pilgrims who go deep in thought." I use "pilgrim" in the larger sense of the word, as it can have two meanings, one broad and the other narrow. Broadly speaking, pilgrims are those traveling outside of their country. More specifically, a pilgrim is one who goes to Santiago de Compostela, burial site of St. James the Apostle, and returns. One should also know that there are three ways to describe people who devote themselves to the service of the Lord. They are called "palmers" when they travel to the Holy Land, because many go there carrying a palm frond or leaf; "pilgrims," when they travel to the house of Galicia, for the sepulchre there of St. James is the most remote of all the apostles' burial sites; and "Romers," when they travel to Rome, which is where those whom I call "pilgrims" were headed.

I do not divide up this sonnet, as its meaning is clear.

O pilgrims who go deep in thought,
Perhaps because of all you miss—
Could your homes be so far away,
As your look leads me to believe,
That you don't weep as you pass through
The middle of this widowed place,
Like those unconscious of the pain
Surrounding them on every side.

If you would pause a while to hear,
My sighing heart reveals to me,
That you would leave this place in tears.
The city's Beatrice, its bliss, is lost,
And any words one says of her
Have force enough to make men weep.

41.

SOON AFTERWARD two ladies asked me to send them
some of my verses. Considering their nobility, I decided
not only to share with them some of my poems, but also
to write a new one in their honor. So I wrote a sonnet
about my condition and sent it along with two others,
"O pilgrims who go deep in thought" and "O come and
listen to my sighs."

The new sonnet begins, "Beyond the sphere," and
has five parts. The first describes the path of my thought,
naming some of its effects. The second tells why it rises
up, and who makes it go there. The third narrates what
I saw there, that is, an honored lady up above. I call this
thought "pilgrim spirit" because it goes up spiritually,
just as pilgrims go outside of their country. The fourth
describes how my thought sees her—that is, what her
nature is—and how my intellect is incapable of under-
standing her. For our intellect is as unable of gazing
upon blessed souls as the eye is of looking into the sun,
according to what the Philosopher, Aristotle, says in the
second book of his *Metaphysics*. The fifth part of the son-
net recounts how inept I am in understanding where my
thought takes me, that is, to her miraculous nature—a
shortcoming that I am at least aware of. I describe how
this all came about because of my lady Beatrice, whose
name I often recall in my thoughts. This fifth part says
"Of this, dear ladies," to show that it is these women to
whom I am speaking. The second part begins, "A new

intelligence"; the third, "And when it hits"; the fourth, "But when it tries"; and the fifth, "I know it tells." I could divide and explain it more subtly, but I think I have said enough and will stop here and not try to gloss it further.

Beyond the sphere with widest arc
Pass sighs that issue from my heart;
A new intelligence, which Love
Has tearfully infused, ascends.
And when it hits upon its mark,
It sees a lady, held so dear.
And through all of her splendid light,
The pilgrim spirit sees her form.
* But when it tries to tell all this,*
I cannot grasp the subtle words
It speaks to the sad heart, its lord.
I know it tells my lady's tale,
As "Beatrice" I often hear—
Of this, dear ladies, I'm aware.

42.

AFTER THIS SONNET there appeared to me a miraculous vision, in which I saw things that made me resolve to say no more about this blessed one until I am capable of describing her more worthily. To get to this point I am studying as much as I can, as my lady truly knows.[111] Should it please Him in which all things live—and if my life were to last long enough—I hope to be able to say things about her[112] that were never said of any other woman. May it please Him who is Lord of all goodness that my soul one day rises to see the glory of His lady— that blessed Beatrice who gloriously gazes into the face of the One who is blessed for all eternity.[113]

NOTES

TRANSLATOR'S PREFACE

1. This opening paragraph on the difficulties of translating Dante's *Commedia* is taken, or adapted, from my essay, "How to Read Dante in the Twenty-First Century," *The American Scholar*, March 22, 2016.

2. I make this point in *Botticelli's Secret: The Lost Drawings and the Rediscovery of the Renaissance* (New York: W. W. Norton, 2022), 169.

3. Examples of Rossetti's archaic lexicon include "thither," "sorely abashed," and "guerdoned in the Great Cycle."

4. For a discussion of the importance of Dante's prose explanations, especially with regard to Dante's relation to Beatrice, see Thomas Stillinger, *The Song of Troilus: Lyric Authority in the Medieval Book* (Philadelphia: University of Pennsylvania Press, 1992), 44–117. In "Text and Document in Dante's *Vita nova*," Dario Del Puppo considers the historical tendency of editors like Boccaccio to marginalize Dante's prose explanations and reformat his poems (*Romanic Review* 112, no. 1 [2021]: 10–23).

5. See Jorge Luis Borges, "*The Divine Comedy*," in *The Poet's Dante*, ed. Peter S. Hawkins and Rachel Jacoff (New York: Farrar, Straus and Giroux, 2001), 126.

6. Helen Vendler remarks that "in the United States we do not say *lady*, we say *woman*." See her review of Andrew Frisardi's translation of the *Vita Nuova*, which Vendler describes as staging a clash between "contemporary American English" and "the archaism of medieval manners" ("The Road to Paradise," *The New Republic*, October 25, 2012).

7. John Milton, "The Verse," in *Paradise Lost*, ed. Gordon Teskey (New York: W. W. Norton, 2020), 3.

8. The seven ways are: *il*, *lo* (each masculine singular); *la* (feminine singular); *l'* (masculine and feminine singular); *i*, *gli* (each masculine plural); and *le* (feminine plural).

INTRODUCTION

9. For a dating of the *Vita Nuova*, see Michelangelo Picone, "*Vita Nuova*," in

The Dante Encyclopedia, ed. Richard Lansing (New York: Garland, 2000), 874–78.

10. Louise Glück, "Vita Nova," in *Vita Nova* (New York: HarperCollins, 1999).

11. Allegra Goodman, "La Vita Nuova," *The New Yorker*, April 26, 2010.

12. This fourfold model of literary interpretation appears in the celebrated "Letter to Cangrande," a guide to *The Divine Comedy* written for the ruler of Verona, Cangrande della Scala, a key patron of Dante. The question of whether or not Dante wrote the text remains an open one. See Robert Hollander, *Dante's Epistle to Cangrande* (Ann Arbor: University of Michigan Press, 1993), 44, 100.

13. For examples of this "essayistic" tradition, see J. E. Shaw, *Essays on the "Vita Nuova"* (Princeton, N.J.: Princeton University Press, 1929); Charles S. Singleton, *An Essay on the "Vita Nuova"* (Cambridge, Mass.: Harvard University Press, 1949); Mark Musa, "An Essay on the *Vita Nuova*," in *Dante's "Vita Nuova*," ed. and trans. Mark Musa (Bloomington: University of Indiana Press, 1973), 87–174; and Jerome Mazzaro, *The Figure of Dante: An Essay on the "Vita Nuova"* (Princeton, N.J.: Princeton University Press, 1981). Giuseppe Mazzotta discusses the word "essay" in relation to the *Vita Nuova* in "The Language of Poetry in the *Vita Nuova*," *Rivista di studi italiani* 1 (1983): 3–14.

14. Robert Pogue Harrison, *The Body of Beatrice* (Baltimore: Johns Hopkins University Press, 1988), 5; see also Harrison's illuminating remarks on the differences between Italian and American critical approaches to the *Vita Nuova* (1–12).

15. For a reading of the scene in relation to the interpretive possibilities it sets in motion, see Harrison, *The Body of Beatrice*, 17.

16. See Giovanni Boccaccio, *Trattatello in Laude di Dante*, ed. Pier Giorgio Ricci, in *Tutte le opere di Giovanni Boccaccio*, vol. 3 (Milan: Mondadori, 1974); English translation, "Life of Dante," in James Robinson Smith, *The Early Lives of Dante*, trans. Philip Wicksteed (London: Alexander Moring, 1904). For a debunking of this alleged meeting on Calendimaggio, May Day, see Marco Santagata, *Dante: The Story of His Life*, trans. Richard E. Dixon (Cambridge, Mass.: Belknap Press/Harvard University Press, 2016), 36. I describe the scene of Dante's first youthful encounter with Beatrice in *Botticelli's Secret: The Lost Drawings and the Rediscovery of the Renaissance* (New York: W. W. Norton, 2022), 24–27.

17. For a discussion of the controversial issue of whether or not Dante and Gemma had a fourth child, named Giovanni, see Santagata, *Dante*, 53.

18. John Keats, *Poems Published in 1820*, ed. M. Robertson (Oxford: Clarendon Press, 1909), 113.

19. Francesca describes how she and Paolo fell into their adulterous embrace after reading *per diletto*, "for pleasure" (*Inferno* 5.127; my trans.) about

Guinevere and Lancelot's stolen kiss and subsequent infidelity. All references to Dante's epic poem are to *La Commedia secondo l'antica vulgata*, ed. Giorgio Petrocchi, Edizione Nazionale della Società Dantesca Italiana, 4 vols. (Milan: Mondadori, 1966–67). Unless otherwise indicated, translations are from Dante, *The Divine Comedy: Inferno, Purgatorio, Paradiso*, trans. Allen Mandelbaum (New York: Everyman's Library, 1995).

20. As Edoardo Sanguinetti writes, Dante's relatively modest upbringing did not stop him "*di frequentare la vita elegante e 'cortese' della città*," "from frequenting the elegant and 'courtly' life of his city" (introduction to Dante, *La Vita Nuova*, ed. Sanguinetti [Milan: Garzanti, 1992], vii).

21. For a study of the ancient and medieval scientific and philosophical traditions informing Cavalcanti's poetry, see Maria Luisa Ardizzone, *Guido Cavalcanti: The Other Middle Ages* (Toronto: University of Toronto Press, 2002).

22. The *dolce stil novo* was never an official movement or school; it was instead a retrospective tag given by Dante in *Purgatorio* 24, to describe the poetry typical of *Vita Nuova*. Here are the words designating this poetic tradition, from Dante's near contemporary Bonagiunta da Lucca to Dante the pilgrim:

> "*O frate, issa vegg' io,*" *diss' elli,* "*il nodo*
> *che 'l Notaro e Guittone e me ritenne*
> *di qua dal* dolce stil novo *ch'i' odo!*" [My emphasis; 55–57]

> "O brother, now I see," he said, "the knot
> that kept the Notary, Guittone, and me
> short of the *sweet new [style]* that I hear.

Two acclaimed masters of the sweet new style, and the ones who drew the most disciples and followers to them, were Cavalcanti and Guido Guinizelli, a Bolognese poet and jurist whom Dante places among the "hermaphrodites," by which he meant those who suffered from an excess of lust, in *Purgatorio*.

23. See Barbara Reynolds, *Dante: The Poet, the Thinker, the Man* (London: I. B. Tauris, 2013), 10.

24. Such was the claim made by Dante's friend and Florentine compatriot Forese Donati in his *tenzone*, poetic duel, with Dante, as described in *Purgatorio* 23. See Dante, "Forese a Dante," in *Rime*, ed. Gianfranco Contini (Turin: Einaudi, 1995), sonnet 88, no. 2, line 8. For background on this renowned *tenzone*, see Taylor Trentadue, "Dante's Friend: Forese Donati, *Tenzone*," Dante's Library, https://sites.duke.edu/danteslibrary/; more broadly, see Fabian Alfie, *Dante's Tenzone with Forese Donati: The Reprehension of Vice* (Toronto: University of Toronto Press, 2011).

25. For a discussion of Dante's relation to Cavalcanti and accompanying bibliography, see Maria Luisa Ardizzone, "Guido Cavalcanti," in Lansing, ed., *The Dante Encyclopedia*, 459–61.

26. For discussion of Dante's cult of the Virgin Mary and its relation to Beatrice, see Peter S. Hawkins, "Dante's 'Poema Sacro': No Either/Or," *Religion and Literature* 42, no. 3 (2010): 147.

27. From *Sonnets and Ballate of Guido Cavalcanti* (London: Stephen Swift, 1912), 29.

28. Jorge Luis Borges, *Nueve ensayos dantescos* (Madrid: EspasaCalpe, 1982).

29. The question of whether Dante was an accomplished visual artist has long vexed scholars. An influential early source, the great Renaissance thinker and Florentine chancellor Leonardo Bruni, wrote that Dante "drew beautifully in his hand." For citation of Bruni's opinion, and evidence that Dante was likely a competent draftsman, see Santagata, *Dante*, 77–79.

30. For a systematic analysis of how often Dante and Beatrice meet in the *Vita Nuova*, see Robert Hollander, "*Vita Nuova*: Dante's Perceptions of Beatrice," *Dante Studies* 92 (1974): 1–18.

31. A. S. Kline, trans., "I visit you daily, and endlessly," Poetry in Translation, 2007, https://www.poetryintranslation.com/PITBR/Italian/Cavalcanti.php.

32. See Cavalcanti's "Noi siàn le triste penne isbigotite," "We are the sad, bewildered quills," trans. Ezra Pound, *The Iowa Review* 12, no. 1 (1981): 47.

33. I explore how Dante's thoughts on the pensive pilgrims helped him reconfigure his idea of his potential readership in "Literary History and Individuality in the *De vulgari eloquentia*," *Dante Studies* 116 (1998): 170.

A NOTE ON THE TEXT

34. For a discussion of the different approaches to the structure of the *Vita Nuova*, see Andrew Frisardi, translator's preface, to Dante Alighieri, *Vita Nova*, trans. Andrew Frisardi (Evanston, Ill.: Northwestern University Press, 2012), xii–xvii. The debates over how to entitle Dante's first book revolve on whether to choose (1) the Latin *nova*, for "new," which Dante finds written in his Book of Memory in chapter 1 ("*Incipit vita nova*," "Here begins the new life"); or (2) the Tuscan *nuova*, for "new." For a study of that key Latin phrase in the *Vita Nuova*, see Alberto Casadei, "Incipit Vita Nova," *Dante Studies* 129 (2011): 179–86. Since Dante's text is emphatically devoted to promoting a new vernacular and dialect literary tradition that could rival ancient Rome's Latin culture, I have opted for the more modern *nuova* for the title.

35. See Paget Toynbee, "The Inquisition and the 'Editio Princeps' of the 'Vita Nuova,'" *Modern Language Review* 3, no. 3 (1908): 229. I discuss this

redacted edition in my *Dante's "Divine Comedy": A Biography* (Princeton, N.J.: Princeton University Press, 2024).

36. See George Watson, "The First English 'Vita Nuova,'" *Huntington Library Quarterly* 49, no. 4 (1986): 401-7.

37. See J. Chesley Mathews, "Emerson's Translation of Dante's 'Vita Nuova,'" *Harvard Library Bulletin* 11, no. 2 (1957): 208-44.

38. English translations that have appeared since the publication of Emerson's include those by Mark Musa (Bloomingon: Indiana University Press, 1973); Barbara Reynolds (London: Penguin, 2004); Stanley Appelbaum (Mineola, N.Y.: Dover, 2006); David R. Slavitt (Cambridge, Mass.: Harvard University Press, 2010); Anthony Mortimer (Richmond, Eng.: Alma Classics, 2011); Frisardi (2012); and Virginia Jewiss (London: Penguin, 2022). For a recent study of the afterlife of the *Vita Nuova* among English readers, see Federica Coluzzi and Jacob Blakesley, eds., *The Afterlife of Dante's "Vita Nova" in the Anglophone World: Interdisciplinary Perspectives on Translation and Reception History* (London: Routledge, 2022).

39. Barbi's division of the text into forty-two chapters was challenged in a seminal study by Guglielmo Gorni, who argued for dividing the work into thirty-one chapters in his edition of the *Vita Nuova* (Turin: Einaudi, 1996). See the discussion in Jewiss's introduction to her translation of Dante, *Vita Nuova*, xix–xx.

VITA NUOVA

40. The original Latin reads: "*Incipit vita nova.*"

41. On the *libello*, little book, of the *Vita Nuova* as one of the first "books" in the Middle Ages, see Ernst Robert Curtius, *European Literature and the Latin Middle Ages*, trans. Willard Trask (Princeton, N.J.: Princeton University Press, 1953), 326–28. More recently, Martin Eisner considers the afterlife of the *Vita Nuova* in a wide array of media and literary forms, tracing its "twisted course of textual transmission" across the centuries (*Dante's New Life of the Book: A Philology of World Literature* [Oxford: Oxford University Press, 2021], 3). For a study of the material creation of Dante's text, see Jelena Todorović, *Dante and the Dynamics of Textual Exchange: Authorship, Manuscript Culture, and the Making of the 'Vita Nova'* (New York: Fordham University Press, 2016).

42. According to Ptolemy and medieval astronomy, the "heaven of the fixed stars" represented the eighth and penultimate sphere surrounding the earth. It was thought to move one degree each century; since one-twelfth of a degree has passed since Beatrice's birth, she is eight years and four months old here. For consideration of Dante's astronomy and its implications for his poetry, see Alison Cornish, *Reading Dante's Stars* (New Haven: Yale University Press, 2000), especially the section on the *Vita Nuova*, 9–20.

43. Dante was born under the sign of Gemini in May or June 1265, while Beatrice, daughter of the eminent banker Folco Portinari, was apparently born a few months later that same year. We have no record of the actual date.

44. Derived from ancient medical sources including Galen, the term "animal spirit" had a precise medical and psychological meaning for Dante and his fellow poets of the sweet new style. As many of their poems reveal—for example, Guido Cavalcanti's magnificent "Donna me prega" ("A lady bids me") and its minute elaboration of love's effect on the human organism—*spiriti*, spirits, are generated in different organs in the body, and each of them has its own particular corporeal function. See Andrew Frisardi, introduction to Dante Alighieri, *Vita Nova*, trans. Andrew Frisardi (Evanston, Ill.: Northwestern University Press, 2012), xliii–xliv: "The natural spirit passes through the veins to the heart, where it is refined into the subtler 'vital spirits.' The vital spirits then circulate in the blood, bringing heat to various parts of the body, and eventually to the brain, where they are further refined and converted into 'animal spirits' (thus called because they are spirits of the *animo*, the mind; i.e., they are mental spirits), or the 'sensible soul.'"

45. The original Latin reads: *"Ecce deus fortior me, qui veniens dominabitur michi."*

46. *"Apparuit iam beatitudo vestra."*

47. *"Heu miser, quia frequenter impeditus ero deinceps!"*

48. Dante could not read Greek, so his likely source here is the *Ilias latina*, a 1,070-line abridgment of the Homeric original into Latin. The reference is probably to *Iliad* 24.58–59, where Hector is described as seemingly divine though he was in fact human-born. Here is Pope's witty rendition from 1720: "But Hector only boasts a mortal claim, / His birth deriving from a mortal dame" (*The Iliad of Homer*, trans. Alexander Pope [New York: American News Company, 1899]).

49. Marco Santagata demurs, arguing that a family of limited means like Dante's could not have afforded separated sleeping quarters for their children. See his *Dante: The Story of His Life*, trans. Richard E. Dixon (Cambridge, Mass.: Belknap Press/Harvard University Press, 2016), 8.

50. *"Ego dominus tuus."* These words recall Yeats's eponymous poem and its gorgeous paraphrase of key moments in the *Vita Nuova*, articulated by the character Ille (who, according to Ezra Pound, was an alter ego of "Willie" or William Butler Yeats himself):

> He [Dante] set his chisel to the hardest stone.
> Being mocked by Guido [Cavalcanti] for his lecherous life,
> Derided and deriding, driven out
> To climb that stair and eat that bitter bread,

He found the unpersuadable justice, he found
The most exalted lady [Beatrice] loved by a man.

William Butler Yeats, "Ego Dominus Tuus," in *The Collected Poems of W. B. Yeats*, ed. Richard Finneran (New York: Scribner, 1996), 160–61, lines 35–40.

51. "*Vide cor tuum.*"

52. The Tuscan term *fedeli d'Amore*, Love's faithful, had a technical resonance for Dante, as it refers to a specific group of friends and fellow poets devoted to the cult of love, as represented by the ominous personified figure. The phrase resurfaces throughout the *Vita Nuova*. One scholar defines the *fedeli d'Amore* as "rare spirits who were struggling to devise a code of life that retained from chivalry the idea of nobility, while making it depend on personal virtue instead of inherited wealth and breeding, and that preserved spiritual aspirations not unlike those of some mendicants without demanding a life of withdrawal or celibacy." William Anderson, *Dante the Maker* (London: Routledge and Kegan Paul, 1980), 80.

53. Three responses to Dante's sonnet have survived: one from Guido Cavalcanti (see *Vita Nuova* 4); another from Cino da Pistoia, who would remain a lifelong friend and pillar of support to Dante during his exile, especially during his stay in Bologna, where Cino received his doctorate in law; and, most bizarrely of all, one from Dante da Maiano, who took a more "medical" approach to Dante's amorous condition, advising him as follows: *"Lavi la tua collia largamente / a ciò che stinga e passi lo vapore / lo qual ti fa favoleggiar loquendo"* ("Wash your testicles thoroughly to quench and dissipate the vapors that are making you speak with such fantasy"). See Dante da Maiano, "Di ciò che stato sè dimandatore" ("The matter you asked me about"), in *Rime*, ed. Rosanna Betterini (Florence: Le Monnier, 1969), 7–9.

54. Dante's *primo amico*, best friend, was Guido Cavalacanti, a figure of profound importance not just in his role as dedicatee of the *Vita Nuova*, but also because of his prominent place in both the history of Italian lyric poetry and—more hauntingly—the composition of Dante's masterpiece, *The Divine Comedy*. A gifted writer who was a superior poet to the younger Dante at the time of *Vita Nuova*'s composition, Cavalcanti was also a polymath, aristocrat, and atheist who authored such groundbreaking works as his signature poem on the phenomenology of love, "A lady bids me" (see above, note 43). Along with Guido Guinizelli, Cavalcanti is considered one of the movement's "founders," though, as I indicated in my introduction (see note 22), that is likely too grand a term for the informal network of poets and lyric production associated with the sweet new style. For Dante's fraught relation with his first poetic mentor, see Robert Pogue Harrison's chapter "The Ghost of Guido Cavalcanti," in *The Body of Beatrice* (Balti-

more: Johns Hopkins University Press, 1988), 69–90. For a volume of Cavalcanti's work in English translation, see Ezra Pound's innovative *Sonnets and Ballate of Guido Cavalcanti* (London: Stephen Swift, 1912).

55. Derived from the Provençal poetry of medieval troubadours, the *sirventese*, "service song," was written in epistolary form (*epistola* derives from the Latin word for "letter") and was generally polemical or satirical in tone, while covering a variety of themes ranging from the political to the religious. In Dante's era, the form evolved to focus on matters of love; Dante's version of it here has not survived.

56. Dante's cult of female beauty also permeates his poem "Guido i' vorrei" ("O Guido, how I wish"). In Shelley's beautiful rendition below, Beatrice appears in the form of her familiar Tuscan nickname, Bice:

> *Guido, I would that Lapo, thou, and I,*
> *Led by some strong enchantment, might ascend*
> *A magic ship, whose charmed sails should fly*
> *With winds at will where'er our thoughts might wend,*
> *And that no change, nor any evil chance*
> *Should mar our joyous voyage; but it might be,*
> *That even satiety should still enhance*
> *Between our hearts their strict community:*
> *And that the bounteous wizard then would place*
> *Vanna and Bice and my gentle love,*
> *Companions of our wandering, and would grace*
> *With passionate talk, wherever we might rove,*
> *Our time, and each were as content and free*
> *As I believe that thou and I should be.*

"Dante Alighieri to Guido Cavalcanti," *The Complete Poetical Works of Percy Bysshe Shelley*, ed. Thomas Hutchinson, vol. 1 (Oxford: Oxford University Press, 1914), https://www.gutenberg.org/cache/epub/4800/pg4800-images.html.

57. Lamentations 1:12.

58. This lightness, *leggiadria*, would become a key term in the Renaissance, suggesting the *sprezzatura*, or seemingly effortless grace, in the work of painters like Botticelli, with all the joy their images suggest. See my *Botticelli's Secret: The Lost Drawings and the Rediscovery of the Renaissance* (New York: W. W. Norton, 2022), 246.

59. This is the first mention of what will be a key term in the *Vita Nuova*: *sospiri*, "sighs."

60. S*bigotito*, "bewildered," was a preeminent signifier in the sweet new style that signaled how the experience of love was a lacerating force.

61. As noted in my introduction to this volume, Dante's use of *cavalcando*, or "riding by horse," is a play on the name Cavalcanti.

62. Dante is playing on the twin meanings of the word *saluto*, as the Italian term indicates both a gesture of greeting and a state of health or well-being.

63. *"Fili mi, tempus est ut pretermicantantur simulacra nostra."*

64. *"Ego tanquam centrum circuli, cui simili modo se habent circumferentie partes; tu autem non sic."*

65. Beatrice's smile would assume a monumental significance in the *Commedia*: Dante will be able to gaze upon it only as his spiritual knowledge grows; in the early stages of his journey through the afterlife with Beatrice, her smile is too overwhelming for him to apprehend. At one point, it is even compared to the lightning bolt of Zeus that burnt his lover Semele to a crisp when she attempted to look at him in his full splendor. As Beatrice remarks, "Were I to smile, then you [Dante] would be / like Semele when she was turned to ashes" (*Paradiso* 21.5–6). For a study of how Beatrice's smile becomes central to Dante's religious knowledge in *The Divine Comedy*, see Rachel Jacoff, "The Post-Palinodic Smile: *Paradiso* VIII and IX," *Dante Studies* 98 (1980): 111–22.

66. The medieval *congedo*, "valediction," was a poetic convention that involved sending a poem out into the world where it would hopefully find well-disposed and accommodating readers.

67. *"Nomina sunt consequentia rerum."*

68. For a medieval poet like Dante, the mention of "the war of these conflicting thoughts" would likely recall the paradigmatic work in this vein, Prudentius's *Psychomachia* (*Battle of Spirits*), a Latin poem from the early fifth century AD that features allegorical struggles between virtues and vices as well as victorious Christian notions and their defeated counterparts—all written in the style of Virgil's *Aeneid*. The term "psychomachy" now refers to a battle within the soul, typically between good and evil.

69. The bodily region referred to is the heart.

70. Calvacanti was magisterial in describing how internal spirits, under the influence of love, can destroy the human agent that houses them. See especially his "Noi siàn le triste penne isbigotite," "We are the sad, bewildered quills":

> the hand that moved us says it feels
> worrying things that have appeared in the heart;
> and these have so destroyed him
> and pushed him so close to death,
> that he has nothing left but sighs.

For the translation, see David Bowe, "Text, Artefact and the Creative Process: 'The Sad, Bewildered Quills' of Guido Cavalcanti," *MHRA: Working Papers in the Humanities* (2015): 11.

71. Dante is using an eminently Cavalcantian signifier here: *spiritelli*, "little spirits."

72. The sonnet is based on a topos of Occitan lyric: the *gabbo* (act of mocking or teasing). For a discussion of this key word in the *Vita Nuova*, see Francesco Flamini, ed., *Le opere minori di Dante Alighieri: Ad uso delle scuole* (Livorno: R. Giusti, 1925), 132*n*.

73. Yet another Cavalcantian lexical choice appears here: *sbigottito*, literally "bewildered" but here translated as "bewitched." See note 70 above for my related discussion of Cavalcanti's "Noi siàn le triste penne *isbigotite*," "We are the sad, *bewildered* quills" (my emphasis on *isbigotite*, a plural variant of *sbigottito*).

74. A canzone, literally "song" in Italian, refers to an Italian or Provençal lyric form, originally comprised of five to seven stanzas, with songlike qualities—hence they were often set to music.

75. One wonders if Petrarch, famously thin-skinned when it came to dealing with Dante's posthumous fame, had this line about how "Love sends a chill" into the heart in mind when he wrote the concluding verses to his lovely madrigal "Non al suo amante più Dïana piacque," "Diana was not more pleasing to her lover": "so that she makes me, now that the *heavens burn*, / tremble, wholly, with the *chill of love*" (my emphasis; trans. A. S. Kline, https://www.poetryintranslation.com/PITBR/Italian/PetrarchCanzoniere001-061.php#anchor_Toc9485190).

76. The mention of public acclaim is important: Dante is by this point slowly expanding the restricted, self-conconsciously elitist circle of his early readership to encompass new groups and currents of literary interest.

77. Dante's line about "love and the gentle heart" recalls the canonical sweet new style poem by Guido Guinizelli, "Al cor gentil rempaira sempre amore," "Love always returns to the gentle heart." Guinizelli's lyric was reprised dramatically by Francesca da Rimini in *Inferno* 5.100 with her line *"Amor ch'al cor gentil ratto s'apprende,"* "Love, that can quickly seize the gentle heart," an example of how her "lustful" imagination was fired by the kind of romantic, erotic verse typical of the *Vita Nuova*.

78. The "sage" in question is Guinizelli.

79. The line echoes the opening of Cavalcanti's haunting poem "Chi è questa che vèn, ch'ogn'om la mira," "Who is she coming, drawing all men's gaze."

80. Here is another potential nod to Cavalcanti's "Chi è questa che vèn" and its line *"Non si poria contar la sua piagenza,"* "Her beauty can't be put in words." For the Dante of *The Divine Comedy*, this topos of ineffability would assume a much more spiritual and religious inflection than the emphasis throughout the earlier *Vita Nuova* on how the experience of love confounds articulate expression.

81. Beatrice's father, Folco Portinari, died on December 31, 1289. A prominent Florentine banker, he attained the city's highest elected office of prior (as Dante would in 1300) several times, and his philanthropy

included the gift of assets to found the Hospital of Santa Maria Nuova in 1288. To this day, it remains Florence's largest and most important medical establishment.

82. *"Osanna in excelsis."*

83. The woman in question was likely Dante's sister Tana.

84. One wonders if this reference to the weeping "sun and star" marinated in Dante's mind when, decades later, he wrote the magnificent concluding verse to the *Commedia*: *"l'amor che move 'l sole e l'altre stelle,"* "the love that moves the sun and the other stars" (*Paradiso* 33.142).

85. The reference is to Guido Cavalcanti, the *primo amico* from *Vita Nuova* 3.

86. *"Ego vox clamantis in deserto: parate viam Domini"* (Matthew 3:3).

87. Dante is using the Aristotelian terminology that would become a staple of medieval Scholastic philosophy. A *sustanza*, substance, exists in itself, whereas an *accidente*, accident, is a property of a substance and thus without an independent life of its own (for example, love is an accident *within* a substance). See the discussion by Anthony Mortimer in his translation of Dante Alighieri, *Vita Nuova* (London: Alma Classics, 2013), 186n. See also the metaphor of the *divino volume*, divine volume, in *Paradiso* 33, when Dante observes the universe as resembling God's grand poem:

> In its profundity I saw—ingathered
> and bound by love into one single volume—
> what, in the universe, seems separate, scattered:
> substances, accidents, *and dispositions*
> as if conjoined—in such a way that what
> I tell is only rudimentary. (My emphasis; 85–90)

88. By "vernacular," Dante means those poets who write in the local Tuscan dialect, a subject that informs his groundbreaking treatise on the Romance languages, *De vulgari eloquentia* (*On Eloquence in the Vernacular*; 1302–5).

89. Hence the mixed prosimetrum form of the *Vita Nuova*, with its challenging blend of poetry and prose.

90. Dante's original reads, *"Eolo, nanque tibi"* (*Aeneid* 1.65). See below, notes 91–95, for Dante's other Latin citations in *Vita Nuova* 25.

91. *"Tuus, O regina, explorare labor; michi iussa capessere fas est"* (*Aeneid* 1.76–77).

92. *"Dardanide duri"* (*Aeneid* 3.94).

93. *"Multum, Roma, tamen debes civilibus armis"* (*Pharsalia* 1.44).

94. *"Dic michi, Musa, virum"* (*Ars poetica* 1.41).

95. *"Bella michi, video, bella parantur, ait"* (*Remedia amoris* 2).

96. Dante seems, once again, to be thinking in Cavalcantian terms about women who reduce their admirers to an unintelligible world of sighs, espe-

cially in his poem "Chi è questa che vèn, ch'ogn'om la mira," "Who is she coming, drawing all men's gaze" (see above, note 79).

97. Jeremiah, in Lamentations 1:1.

98. In a moving testament to the resurgence of Dante's popularity during the Romantic era, the merchant and author Edward Quillinan quoted this line from the *Vita Nuova* on the eve of the death of his wife, Dora, the daughter of the poet William Wordsworth, in 1847:

> My Beloved Dora breathed her last at one o'clock A. M.—less five minutes by the stairclock at Rydal Mount.—*Io dico che l'anima sua nobi[l]issima si partì nella prima ora del nono giorno del mese.* "I say that her most noble soul departed in the first hour of the ninth day of the month." Dante. Vita Nuova. Beatrice.

From Quillinan's Journal, Wordsworth Library; courtesy of Dove Cottage, Wordsworth Trust. I discuss Quillinan's diary entry and its broader implications in my *Romantic Europe and the Ghost of Italy* (New Haven: Yale University Press, 2008), 141; and in *Botticelli's Secret*, 155–56.

99. Beatrice Portinari died in 1290.

100. In the medieval version of the Ptolemaic system, an outer sphere was believed to circle the earth in twenty-four hours, carrying the inner spheres with it.

101. See the opening of *Vita Nuova* 28.

102. A harrowing echo of these words would appear in *Inferno* 33, when the desperate Ugolino narrates to Dante the chain of events that landed him in deepest hell—and may very well have compelled him to eat the bodies of his dead children:

> *Ma se le mie parole esser dien seme*
> *che frutti infamia al traditor ch'i' rodo,*
> parlar e lagrimar *vedrai* insieme.

> But if my words are seed from which the fruit
> is infamy for this betrayer whom
> I gnaw, you'll see me *speak and weep at once.* (My emphasis; 7–9)

103. The reference to "heart of stone" recalls the so-called *rime petrose*, stony rhymes, that Dante wrote to a cold and unresponsive woman around 1296, soon after completing the *Vita Nuova*. For a chronological sequencing of the *rime petrose*, see Teodolinda Barolini, introduction to Dante Alighieri, *Dante's Lyric Poetry: Poems of Youth and of the "Vita Nuova" (1283–1292)*, ed. Teodolinda Barolini, trans. Richard Lansing (Toronto: University of Toronto Press,

NOTES TO PAGES 114–127 | 149

2014), 4; and for a reading of the *rime petrose* centered on the heart's physical and poetic implications for Dante's poetry, see Heather Webb, "Dante's Stone Cold Rhymes," *Dante Studies* 121 (2003): 149–68. For a general study, see Robert M. Durling and Ronald L. Martinez, *Time and the Crystal: Studies in Dante's* Rime petrose (Berkeley: University of California Press, 1990).

104. See Francesca da Rimini's similar rhetoric of her lover's face drained of blood and color in *Inferno* 5:

> *Per più fiate li occhi ci sospinse*
> *quella lettura, e* scolorocci il viso;
> *ma solo un punto fu quel che ci vinse.*

> And time and time again that reading led
> our eyes to meet, and *made our faces pale*,
> and yet one point alone defeated us. (My emphasis; 130–32)

105. Dante's second best friend was most likely Manetto Portinari, one of Beatrice's five brothers.

106. For a discussion of Dante as "artist," see note 29.

107. This line, which in the original reads, *"Amor, che ne la mente la sentia,"* recalls Dante's acclaimed canzone "Amor che nella mente mi ragiona," "Love that reasons in my mind," which Dante's friend the musician Casella performed for a group of rapt listeners—including Dante the pilgrim—before stern Cato broke up the impromptu recital and sent the penitents back on their road of purgation (see *Purgatorio* 2.112–14). For a discussion of how this canzone, which would later be central to Dante's philosophical magnum opus the *Convivio* (*Banquet*; 1304–7), fits into Dante's larger practice of self-citation and autobiography, see Teodolinda Barolini, *Dante's Poets: Textuality and Truth in the* Comedy (Princeton, N.J.: Princeton University Press, 1984), 40–57.

108. This *donna gentile*, "gentle lady," will reappear as the muse of the *Convivio*. For a discussion of this major figure in Dante's poetic career, see Peter Dronke, *Dante's Second Love: The Originality and Contexts of the "Convivio"* (London: Routledge, 1997), especially chapter 1, "From Beatrice to the Donna Gentile," 1–25. See also Olivia Holmes's discussion of how Dante's choice between "two women" like Beatrice and the gentle lady of the *Vita Nuova* carried profound ethical implications, in her *Dante's Choice and Romance Narratives of Two Beloveds* (New Haven: Yale University Press, 2008), especially chapter 1, "Two Ways and Two Ladies," 13–35.

109. The line *"Tu vedi che questo è uno spiramento d'Amore,"* "You are witnessing Love's inspiration," plays on the Latin root of the word *inspirare*, "to breathe into"—an etymology that Dante would skillfully exploit in his celebrated naming of the sweet new style in *Purgatorio* 24:

E io a lui: "I' mi son un che, quando
Amor mi spira, noto, e a quel modo
ch'e' ditta dentro vo significando."

I answered: "I am one who, *when Love breathes*
in me, takes note; what he, within, dictates,
I, in that way, without, would speak and shape." (My emphasis; 52–54)

110. The phrase *"ragiona d'amor sì dolcemente,"* "speak of love with words so sweet," will be reprised by Dante in line 12 of "Guido i' vorrei" (see above, note 56), which describes how Dante and his friends Cavalcanti and Lapo Gianni would set sail on a magic boat, *"e quivi ragionar sempre d'amore,"* "and here speak always of love."

111. Crucially, the *Vita Nuova* transitions to the present tense here, to signify that the two "Dantes"—the protagonist of the text and its author—are now one and the same, as the retrospective narration of the *Vita Nuova* culminates in these final words and thoughts in the living present.

112. The question of whether this dramatic conclusion—that Dante will say no more of Beatrice until he can do so in a more majestic manner—points to the eventual genesis of *The Divine Comedy*, some ten years later, is a complicated one. Many are persuaded, understandably, by the sheer romance and poetry of the interpretation that Dante was in fact implicitly pointing toward his magnum opus, the *Commedia*, with this promise to hold his literary tongue until it was more qualified to speak of Beatrice. Despite its obvious seductions, I cannot accept this view: *The Divine Comedy* is a deeply religious work, with a completely different Beatrice than the one in the *Vita Nuova*. In fact, in *Purgatorio* 30, when Dante meets Beatrice for the first time in the poem, she actually rebukes him for daring to speak of her in the lovestruck tones and rhetoric that recall the *Vita Nuova*. Of course, when Dante concluded the *Vita Nuova* sometime between 1292 and 1295, he could not have known of his impending exile in 1302 and the oceanic political turmoil that was about to upend his life. More than his love for Beatrice, I believe that the experience of exile and the spiritual crisis that likely grew out of it are the primary engines for the birth of the *Commedia*. Dante's conclusion to the *Vita Nuova* is thus both beautiful and unwittingly prophetic; but it does not, in my view, suggest or imply that he had a "plan" for writing of Beatrice in a work as grand as the *Commedia*. For a thoughtful consideration of the issue, see Colin Hardie, "Dante's 'Mirabile Visione' (*Vita Nuova* xlii)," in *The World of Dante: Essays on Dante and His Times*, ed. Cecil Grayson (Oxford: Clarendon Press, 1980), 123–45.

113. Dante's Latin original for "who is blessed for all eternity" reads: *"qui est per omnia secula benedictus."*